"I didn't decide to be single. A good man just hasn't come along yet, that's all," Marlo told Jenny.

"What about the Cinderella List?" her sister pointed out. "Does a man with your requirements even exist?"

"It was just a *game*, Jen...." Though Marlo wondered when it had turned into something more in her mind.

Jenny slipped out of the room, and returned some minutes later with a piece of folded white typing paper in her hand. "Here. I jotted this down. Maybe it will clarify things for you."

What was Jenny up to now?

The Ideal Man According to Marlo Mayfield

- *Handsome (da̶*
- *Good teeth, g̶*
- *Well educated*
- *Good manner̶*
- *Earns a dece̶*
- *Looks good in jeans and c̶*
- *Thoughtful, compassionate, intuitive*
- *Sense of humor*
- *Faith in God*

Could love be far behind?

Books by Judy Baer

Love Inspired

Be My Neat-Heart
Mirror, Mirror
Sleeping Beauty
The Cinderella List

Steeple Hill Single Title

The Whitney Chronicles
Million Dollar Dilemma
Norah's Ark

JUDY BAER

"Angel" Award-winning author and two-time RITA®
Award finalist Judy Baer has written more than
seventy books in the past twenty years. A native of
North Dakota and graduate of Concordia College
in Minnesota, she currently lives near Minneapolis.
In addition to writing, Judy works as a personal life
coach and writing coach. Judy speaks in churches,
libraries, women's groups and at writers' conferences
across the country. She enjoys time with her husband,
two daughters, three step children and the growing
number of spouses, pets and babies they bring home.
Judy, who once raised buffalo, now owns horses. She
recently completed her master's degree and accepted
a position as adjunct faculty at St. Mary's University,
Minneapolis, MN. Readers are invited to visit her
Web site at www.judykbaer.com.

The Cinderella List
Judy Baer

Steeple
Hill®
Published by Steeple Hill Books™

STEEPLE HILL BOOKS

Steeple
Hill®

Recycling programs
for this product may
not exist in your area.

ISBN-13: 978-0-373-87594-8

THE CINDERELLA LIST

www.SteepleHill.com

Printed in U.S.A.

He who finds a wife finds a good thing,
and obtains favor from the Lord.
—*Proverbs* 18:22

For Tom, who fulfills all the requirements
for my Prince Charming!

Chapter One

"Mr. Hammond was very explicit that he wanted us there on time. Successful men are like that." The catering van took a right turn so sharply that Marlo Mayfield grabbed the handle above her door and hung on tightly. Marlo and her business partner, Lucy Morten, rushed to set up tonight's catering job.

"Stop signs are not a suggestion, Lucy. They are an order." Dressed in a pale blue blouse, with a Dining with Divas logo on it, Marlo tentatively let go of the handle and hoped for the best.

She studied the neighborhood through which they were driving. Lucy was right about their client's success. No one lived in a neighborhood like this without a thriving business, a spot on a professional sports team or a hefty trust fund.

They drove up to a huge, castlelike English Tudor home. Sloping lawns led away from the house toward a maze of low shrubbery and a man-made pond. Statuary fountains of maidens carrying jugs were pouring water into the pool. There were seating-area vignettes scattered around the velvety grass, teak chairs and tables with brightly colored umbrellas and wrought-iron sets decorated with vases of flowers.

This was her dream home, Marlo marveled, the one she'd drawn sketches of in the backs of her notebooks as a child. Of course, in *her* drawings, a knight in shining armor always stood guard at the front gate. And she'd always depicted herself entering at the front of the house, not the service entrance, where they were headed.

"Are we serving outside? The lawn looks like a movie set." Marlo expected F. Scott Fitzgerald's Gatsby and his gang to stroll by any moment.

"No. The party is on the main floor of the house. Not every yard is a lawn ornament graveyard like yours," Lucy commented absently.

Marlo had inherited a plaster donkey pulling a cart full of fake geraniums, and a windmill that tipped over in every breeze, from her great-aunt Tildy, who didn't like them well enough to leave them in her own yard.

"You must really love your aunt a lot," Lucy commented. "I wouldn't keep that stuff around, even for my own grandmother!"

"She's like a second mom to me," Marlo said.

Marlo didn't mention to Lucy how flattering it had been to be told that she resembled her aunt Tildy when she was young. That was the highest compliment someone in Marlo's family could receive. Tall, slender, gorgeous, and with a figure anyone in senior living would give a molar to have, Tildy was the classic independent spirit. Marlo, her father often said, was the mirror image of his sister when she was young. Tildy, according to family lore, had more than once literally stopped traffic with her looks.

"Aunt Tildy has flair. She marches to no one's drummer but her own."

"She sounds a lot like you." Lucy spied the door she was looking for and made a sharp left, nearly pitching Marlo into the driver's seat. Then she slammed the brake to the floor and the van stopped with a shudder by an open wooden door. Ivy crept up the bricks around it and through the screen Marlo could see the stainless steel accoutrements of a professional kitchen.

As they carried the first trays through the open door, Marlo stared at the commercial quality appliances, granite countertops and the glass doors on the Sub-Zero refrigerator.

There were really only five things in life that Marlo longed for— a close relationship with God, a life partner, a successful business, to make a difference in the world—and a kitchen like this one.

But this was no time for daydreams. She immediately began to organize multitiered platters of finger foods, tarts and hot trays for wings and sausage-stuffed mushrooms. Lucy finished the dessert buffet.

"Can you imagine what we could do if we had this kitchen?" she asked rhetorically, not expecting Lucy to answer. "The business we could generate?" She loved making new plans for their catering business. Some worked, some didn't. Offering a dessert buffet was a hit with their clients. The sushi to go? Everyone loved it. Fiber-rich chocolate cake? Not so much.

She walked across the room to where a series of framed black-and-white photos hung over the banquette in a small sitting area on one side of the kitchen. That and inviting, red, upholstered wing chairs, plush red, black and cream area rugs and stately porcelain horse sculptures seemed to be waiting for the master to arrive home after the hunt. An open Bible—obviously well read— lay on a mahogany end table, a sight that warmed her heart.

She moved gracefully into the niche, running a finger over the soft leather of the banquette. "I'd sit here to choose recipes for the night's dinner—scampi maybe, or a nice tortellini with red sauce…."

While Marlo drifted into her Barefoot Contessa fantasy, Lucy stared at the photos on the wall. "Magnificent," she breathed. "Absolutely magnificent."

Lucy usually saved that kind of praise for cakes with rolled fondant icing, so Marlo was surprised to peer over her shoulder and realize that she was looking at the black-and-white portraits of gleaming, powerfully built—and, yes, magnificent—horses.

There were horsey things subtly scattered elsewhere: a needle-point pillow on one of the chairs boasted a muscular black horse; embroidered delicately onto hems of the luxurious red-and-cream curtains was a stylized rendition of the head of a stallion.

"I always wanted a horse," Marlo said wistfully. "But we lived in the city and there was never any money to board a pony back then. My bedroom was papered with pictures of horses I'd cut out of magazines, drawn or colored. Mother said I preferred whinnying to talking and wanted to eat oatmeal three times a day after I learned horses ate oats. Can you imagine?"

"You must have been a very odd child."

"My sister and I were *both* odd children, if you ask me. When I wasn't thinking about horses, which I knew little or nothing about, we lived in a world of pink castles, party dresses and charming princes. We were the most girly girls you'd ever want to meet. We played dress-up and walked around on the arms of imaginary princes."

Though she didn't admit it, those childhood fantasies had made a lasting imprint on her view of the world. She still believed that handsome, gallant princes did exist—somewhere. Unfortunately, she hadn't run into any of them yet.

"In a six-year-old mind, what qualities does a good Prince Charming have?"

Marlo grinned and her eyes sparkled. "Mine always smelled like oatmeal-raisin cookies."

Ever since Marlo and Jenny had seen the movies *Cinderella*

and *Snow White and the Seven Dwarfs,* they'd played a private little game about the traits they each would require of their own future Prince Charming. In their tween years it was things like a driver's permit and playing on junior varsity. It was a silly childhood joke that she and her sister still occasionally revisited, tongue in cheek. To the list of requirements for their ideal man, they'd since added a 401K and health insurance.

"We called it 'the Cinderella List.'" Marlo smiled at the memory of those two little girls, pencils in hand, somberly devising the List. "It's changed a lot over the years. When I was a kid, my Prince Charming had to have enough money to buy me candy, be able to ride a two-wheeler and wear a baseball cap.

"As a teenager, I wanted him to have a cool car, play football and get along with my parents. As I matured, so did my list. I still remember the last list Jenny and I concocted. It was pretty good, if I remember correctly."

"And you're still looking for a man with the qualities on that list?"

"Like I said, it was a good list. Too bad I didn't use it a few years ago." Marlo obliquely referred to her former Prince Charming, who turned out to be a royal toad. "By now we've refined the list so much that a man doesn't exist who can fulfill it."

"I'm going to ask Jenny about this."

"You've got better things to do, Lucy, like figuring out where to place the ice sculpture. By the look of this house, we should have ordered one in the shape of a horse. Most people have pictures of their children on their walls. Makes you wonder, doesn't it?"

Marlo sank onto the arm of one of the big chairs. Her expression grew pensive and her large blue eyes unfocused. "I like daydreaming about the people who own the houses in which we work. What are their interests? How did they get where they are? Are they happy?"

"You spend too much time with your head in the clouds." Lucy grabbed a dish towel and began to wipe the counter. "Still, that creative part of you comes in handy. It amazes me how you can toss the most unlikely foods together and make them taste so good. It's an art."

"I imagine a taste on my tongue, and then I work backward until I find the right combination of food and spices to make it happen, that's all."

The expression on Lucy's features implied that it was a strange gift Marlo enjoyed.

Marlo ignored her, to concentrate on dishes of olives and pearl onions. Then the door opened and suddenly the fantasy man, the personification of the List she and Jenny had imagined for her all these years, walked into the kitchen.

Chapter Two

He was gorgeous. Literally.

Here he was, the personification of that tuxedoed dream man she and Jenny had concocted, smiling and casually sampling a deviled egg. In her dreams, Marlo's perfect man always wore a tuxedo. That, according to her father, was her mother's fault. Mrs. Mayfield had watched a lot of old Cary Grant movies while she was pregnant.

She could feel her heart pounding and her throat went dry. The response was so abrupt and powerful that it almost frightened her. Even when she'd discovered Jeremiah had betrayed her, her body hadn't reacted as strongly.

Marlo considered herself generally coolheaded but this…this was the guy on the white horse, wearing the armor, rescuing her from the dragon. Suddenly the joke she and Jenny had shared all these years didn't seem quite so funny. Of course, she'd never expected the man from her imagination to turn up before her very eyes.

"I see the housekeeper left the door open for you. Dining with Divas, I presume?" Her fantasy dreamboat stood framed in the doorway, his elegant, chiseled features lit in the golden glow of lights in the other room, his back to the richly paneled room behind him where an honest-to-goodness butler was standing as straight and still as one of the Queen's guards.

As he stepped into the kitchen, Marlo could see more clearly the even profile and the amused grin that played on his lips. He wore his hair short, but not short enough to tame the natural curl that evidenced itself above his ears and at the nape of his neck. She gawked at the perfectly polished shoes, his strong hands and even, charming smile. Fortunately, he didn't appear to notice.

"Your catering business has a very good reputation." There was pleasant anticipation in his honeyed tone and his brown eyes twinkled. "I'm expecting great things tonight."

A pleasant shiver worked its way through Marlo as she recovered from her initial shock. Granted, this fellow looked like her dream man, but there was much more to her idea of the perfect mate than looks. She'd dated handsome men in the past and learned that the hard way. In fact, the most handsome man she'd ever loved had hurt her the most.

He looked at the women's dumbstruck expressions and smiled more widely still, his white, even smile appearing more amused than apologetic. "Sorry, I forgot to introduce myself. I'm Jake Hammond. I'm part-owner of Hammond Stables. You're catering a get-together for some of our clients tonight."

"Stables?" Lucy's round, ingenuous face looked confused. "I thought someone from a place called HMD set up this engagement."

"HMD is Hammond, Mercer and Devins, an architectural firm. That's my day job. Hammond Stables is my hobby."

Horses, Marlo knew, were a hobby like sailing in the America's Cup—neither easy nor cheap.

He eyeballed a plate of Marlo's specialty, a hot artichoke dip, picked up a cracker and a knife and took a sample. Marlo watched raptly, glad she hadn't been skimpy with the artichokes. Who knew her hot artichoke dip would pass through the lips of an Adonis like this?

She couldn't tear her gaze from him. As an incurable romantic, enthralled with those Cinderella fairy tales even into her teens, Marlo had sketched dreamy renditions of a guy like this all over her high-school notebooks. And now here he was, come to life and eating her artichoke dip. *Appreciates fine food. Check.* It didn't get much better than this. He probably even smelled like oatmeal-raisin cookies.

"I-is there anything else you'd like us to do right now?" she stammered.

"You're doing just fine." He winked and Marlo's knees nearly liquefied. That debonair look combined with a playful smile, shades of *North by Northwest* and *To Catch a Thief.* "And no doubt you'll be as glad as I will to have this stuffy event over."

He's so handsome it should be illegal, she thought grumpily. *Somebody should be prosecuted for looking like that, running around giving women heart attacks and all.* Still, she didn't draw her gaze away.

"Jake, darling? What are you doing in the kitchen? The guests are arriving." A beautiful blonde woman in an strapless, emerald silk taffeta dress rustled into the room. Her skin was flawless porcelain and her lips full and pouty. She appeared coy, brazen and petulant all at once. "Your father, grandfather and his friends are looking for you. The Hammond triumvirate is to gather in the hall to welcome guests."

She looked at Lucy and Marlo, in their black-and-white serving clothes and sensible shoes. "You hired these people to take care of things. Now let them."

At first Hammond didn't seem inclined to jump to the beauty's bidding, but then thought better of it, and with a generous smile at Marlo and Lucy, he turned and held out his hand. The young blonde curled herself kittenishly around his arm as they walked out of the kitchen and returned to the party.

"He's too good-looking to be real," Lucy said, sinking into a chair. "I'll bet he's a hologram or something."

"You watch too much TV."

"Too bad he's taken." She looked slyly at Marlo. "You aren't seeing anyone right now. Unfortunately, that blonde had her paws all over him."

"They make a lovely couple."

"He'd be perfect for you. I wish you'd start dating again. You are simply too fussy about men. Charlie was a nice guy." Lucy scowled. "Maybe it's that dumb list of yours."

Lucy referred to Marlo's latest ex-flame. Marlo felt no regret at encouraging Charlie to date other women or the fact that he'd actually become engaged to one of them. They would never have made it as a couple.

He'd gone to church with her. He'd attended Bible study with her. But he'd been going only to please her. None of it meant much to him—other than the fact it was a way to make points with her. That didn't work for Marlo. Charlie needed to do those things for himself, and until he did they couldn't be on the same wavelength. If the spiritual connection wasn't in place, then a romantic relationship wouldn't work either. Sincere, active faith was the first item on the Cinderella List, and there would be no negotiation there. When she checked that item off her list, it had to be for real.

"Charlie needs to have his own relationship with God. I'm not a proxy who can do it for him."

"At least you aren't like most of the single women I know." Lucy plucked a stray radish from a plate of crudités. "You don't talk nonstop about your biological clock."

"Unfortunately, I think mine ran out of batteries, got un-plugged or something. I wish I could find a man who could jump-start it for me."

"You probably have Jeremiah Cole to thank for that."

Tall, blond, tan, rugged in a surfer sort of way, he'd swept her off her feet the first time they met. She only found out later that he, with his compelling green eyes and smooth words, had a way of sweeping *many* women off their feet.

It had been a dreadful time. Marlo had been planning her own fairy-tale wedding—and might even have gone through with it, had she not caught her fiancé and his "other woman" in a cozy tête-à-tête in a downtown hotel restaurant. She knew for sure what it felt like to have a broken heart—one shattered like a piece of brittle glass.

Marlo despised revisiting that time in her life, but it was im-possible to avoid sometimes, especially when someone new ex-pressed a romantic interest in her. The experience had colored every relationship she'd had since, and her views not only about immoral men, but about soulless women who were willing to step into an existing relationship and break it apart.

"I learned a few things back then, Lucy. It wasn't all wasted."

What she had learned was that men were not to be fully trusted, because they could be comfortably engaged to one woman and dating another. She also learned that no matter how much she cared about someone, she would never pursue him if there was someone else in his life. She learned that the last thing she would ever be was the other woman.

It was painful even now, months after the breakup. "I thought that we'd be perfect together, and look what a mess that turned out to be. This time I'll wait for God to handpick someone right for me, and stay out of the selection process."

"Admirable," Lucy said. "It's *going* to take an act of God to find someone for you. I worry that the standards you've set for your ideal mate are so high that no one will ever match your qualifications. You'll regret that Cinderella List of yours.

"Jake Hammond is a perfect match in the physical looks category. Did you see what happens to his eyes when he smiles? They crinkle up and practically *dance* with laughter." Lucy gazed dreamily into the glass-fronted refrigerator, swollen with food they'd transferred from the coolers in the van. "And you could hardly miss the way he fills out a suit. He must lift weights, don't you think?"

Marlo thrust a tassle-topped toothpick into a meatball and handed Lucy the tray. "Scram. These go to the table."

"If I can't think about men, I can still imagine living in this house and cooking in this kitchen," Lucy continued. "The parties we could have. Elegant, sophisticated…crème brûlée at every meal…truffles…caviar…sushi…."

"Crème brûlée at every meal? I don't know." Marlo tapped her finely shaped chin with a fingernail, as if trying to imagine it. Simultaneously, they looked at the clock on the kitchen wall. "Let's party."

Every time Marlo entered the vast dining and living room areas of the house to refill plates, her eyes scanned the room for Jake. The consummate host, he continually circled the room, speaking to every single guest as he moved. She noticed, however, that there was one guest who received more of Jake's attention than the rest. An elderly woman with snow-white hair, pink cheeks and miles of wrinkles etching her face made her way slowly across the room, leaning heavily on a burled wood cane. She reminded Marlo of Britain's Queen Mum. When she approached a group, conversation slowed and those in the group became very deferential, almost obsequious. Only when she left would they start their animated chatter again.

Jake, however, didn't show the same reverence for the old woman. Each time he came around to her, their heads bent together, dark and white, and he would whisper something in her ear that made her smile. Curiosity ate at Marlo. What was their relationship? she wondered. What could a pair like that have in common?

About halfway through the evening, Marlo found out. The kitchen door opened and the regal little woman entered, surreptitiously escorted by Jake.

"I don't think they saw us leave," Jake said.

The old woman bobbed her head. "Good. That's the stuffiest crowd I've been around in a long time." She looked at Marlo, who was staring slack-jawed at the pair. "Jake said you'd make me a sandwich. I haven't had supper and no amount of finger food will fill me up like a peanut butter and banana sandwich will. Jake will join me."

Jake moved to the cupboard and took out the ingredients. He held up a banana from a fruit bowl on the counter. "Do you mind?"

Marlo stifled a laugh. "Of course not. Do you have any preferences? Thick chunks of banana? Thin?"

"Thick," he and Bette said in unison.

As the caterer began to prepare the sandwiches, Jake said, "This is Bette Howland, grand dame of the horse world in these parts. She's also my godmother and one of my best friends."

"Nice to meet you. I'm Marlo Mayfield." She took a plate of sandwiches to the table. "Milk?"

Bette looked at Jake with a twinkle in her eye. "A woman who can cook. You should be nice to this one, Jake." Eyeing the attractive caterer, Jake couldn't disagree.

"Too many of these pretty young things after Jake are useless in the kitchen. Don't know how they get by with it, but it's shameful. Don't they know the way to a man's heart is through his stomach?"

Bette turned again to him. "Right?"

"Absolutely." Jake smiled, glad to spend a few minutes with Bette, away from the gathering in the other room. But after gulping down a half a sandwich, he pushed away from the table. Realizing he should get back to the party, he said, "Bette, I'll come and get you in a few minutes."

The elderly woman waved a sandwich in the air as if to shoo him away. "Take your time, dearie," she said, watching Jake leave.

Bette turned her bright eyes and full attention on Marlo.

"You're a pretty thing. Jake could do much worse than you."

Marlo felt a blush burning up from her neck. "I'm just the caterer."

Bette snorted. "That has nothing to do with anything. Jake doesn't have a pretentious bone in his body, unlike his father, I might add. Jake is like his grandfather, Samuel, my brother." Her expression softened. "Those two are cut of the same cloth—compassionate, fair, loving. And Jake, bless his heart, puts up with a crotchety old woman like me." She lowered her voice. "We go out on *dates,* you know."

She grinned at Marlo's puzzled expression. "Movies no one else thinks I should see—action-adventure mostly, suspense, mystery. Gory ones sometimes, although Jake refuses to take me to a horror movie. He's afraid I might like them. Then we eat at a little diner around the corner from the movie theater. Oh, the heartburn I get!" Bette said happily. "I just love that boy."

The old woman's eyes turned sly. "I think you'd love him, too."

Marlo didn't doubt it. Bette had just described a man that fit perfectly with the List. Unfortunately, that was Jake's decision, not Bette's.

At that moment the kitchen door burst open. "Come on, Bette, let's stroll back in like we've never been gone," Jake said. Bette jumped to her feet as though that cane of hers was a mere prop, and they vanished together into the din in the other room.

A big grin spread across her face. She liked Jake Hammond.

Two hours later, Marlo and Lucy were eyeing the last of the meatballs, a single plate of veggies and dip and the empty trays they'd stacked on the kitchen counter.

If the guests didn't quit eating soon, they would run out of food. Hammond had told Lucy there would be twenty or thirty people in attendance, but there were at least fifty. Marlo hoped they had cans of smoked oysters in the van. Perhaps they could do something with them on a cracker.

As she planned their next move, the kitchen door swung open and Jake strode in. His tie was loosened and pulled to one side, the top button of his shirt open, as if he'd worked up a sweat entertaining the crowd. "I had no idea I'd invited a plague of locusts to this party," he said apologetically, his eyes warm with sympathy, "but they love your food. The guests are leaving with truffles in their pockets and sushi in their purses."

He grinned impishly and a slash of appealing dimple appeared in one cheek. His skin tone was that of an outdoorsman, tan and healthy-looking, not the pasty look of an office-dwelling architect. "My reputation as high-class host is sealed, thanks to you." With a thumbs-up, he disappeared again into the din in the main room.

"That was thoughtful," Lucy commented. "It was as if he read our minds."

"Not mine." Marlo tapped a finger to her temple. "There's nothing up here to read."

"Reading *your* mind is like trying to read a newspaper while riding a Tilt-a-Whirl," Lucy said cheerfully. "There's too much happening at once to make any sense of it."

Marlo wasn't sure she liked the analogy, even if it was apt, but she didn't have time to debate the statement. She and Lucy needed to make the serving trays and platters discreetly disappear in the next few minutes.

By eleven, the kitchen was spotless and most of the guests had taken their leave, except for Sabrina the kittenish blonde attached to Jake by Super Glue. Marlo had watched them all evening, as she moved in and out of the main rooms refilling trays and removing dishes. There was something so engaging about Jake Hammond that she couldn't tear her eyes from him.

As if thinking of them actually conjured them up, they walked into the kitchen looking like a pair of dolls, Soiree Sabrina and her boyfriend, Tuxedo Jake.

"I've called you a cab," Hammond was telling Sabrina as they entered.

She pouted. "I'm not done partying yet, darling."

"Then you'll have to find someone else," Hammond advised her pleasantly, his charm not slipping for an instant. "I'm out of steam."

"But you promised—" Her words were cut short by the sharp blast of a horn.

"Cab's here. Come on, sweets, I'll tuck you in and pay the fare." Smoothly, Hammond navigated his reluctant package toward the door.

Chivalrous. Check.

Only moments after they'd left, the door swung open again and the party's other host, Randall Hammond, strode into the room. The senior Hammond was shorter than his son by two or three inches, strong-looking but thin and sinewy, like, Marlo mused, a piece of human beef jerky. There was a hardness about the man, an inflexible, unbending quality, totally unlike that of his son. As much as Marlo had liked Jake upon first meeting him, she felt conversely wary of his father.

But perhaps she'd judged too quickly, since the first words

out of his mouth were a compliment. "Well done. My guests appreciated your hard work." His pale eyes darted around the room. "Is Jake…"

"He's outside. He sent for a cab and…"

"He's sending Sabrina home in a cab? Odd. He always drives her home." The older Hammond appeared puzzled. "Those two usually close down every party. What a pair they make." He looked both pleased and paternal at the notion.

Another man of Randall's age strolled through the kitchen door. He held the hand of a child with bright eyes, a curious expression on her perfectly oval face and a mass of blond curls cascading down her back.

Marlo couldn't remember the last time she'd seen a child so beautiful.

"It's time to get you home to bed, Cammi."

"Not so soon, Grandpa. I don't have school tomorrow." She released her grandfather's hand and skipped to the glass-fronted refrigerator and pressed her nose against the glass. "I've never been in this part of the house before. It's fun."

"Your grandmother never uses that adjective to describe her kitchen, I'm afraid," the child's grandfather said, with a chuckle. "I'm not sure that she's even visited her kitchen lately, except for the occasional glass of water or to harass a caterer or two."

"Oh, Grandpa!" Cammi chided. "I'm telling."

"Don't you dare, little miss." He leaned down to pick her up and the child wrapped her arms around his neck. "Your grandmother will insist on coming along on our dates if she thinks we're having too much fun. Besides, if your aunt Sabrina has already left, you know we've certainly overstayed our welcome!"

The child giggled and buried her nose in her grandfather's

collar. The little girl already possessed some of Sabrina's stunning good looks. It must be nice to be part of such a genetically blessed clan, Marlo mused.

"Ladies," Randall Hammond said, "this is my friend, Alfred Dorchester, and his beautiful granddaughter Cammi."

Alfred smiled pleasantly and tipped his head. "Nice to meet you." Cammi, still smarting from her grandfather's refusal to stay any later, remembered her manners and mumbled, "Hello."

Alfred's gaze found that of the older Hammond. "Randall, I just came to tell you that Cammi and I are leaving. I'll stop by the stables tomorrow."

"Me, too?" Cammi put the palms of her hands on her grandfather's cheeks. "Can I come, too?" Seeing her grandfather hesitate, she turned to the elder Hammond. "Can I?"

Randall Hammond fondly stroked one of the child's long, tight curls with his forefinger. "If you do, you can see our new colts," he offered. It was clear that both men adored this beautiful child.

"Unless your mother doesn't want you to be a tomboy tomorrow."

Cammi wrinkled her nose. "Bor—ring."

Laughing, the men exited the kitchen. Only the little girl, looking back over her grandfather's shoulder, waved an acknowledging goodbye to Marlo and Lucy.

Jake returned immediately to the kitchen after tucking Sabrina into a cab, his interest piqued by the long-legged, dark-haired, blue-eyed beauty in the kitchen. It wasn't often that someone so appealing or charismatic showed up in his life. He was accustomed to beautiful and sophisticated women, but this one displayed a good-natured charm that captivated him.

"Your father and his friend were just in here looking for you," the lovely caterer informed him, as she expertly packed used glasses in carrying containers.

"Alfred? Did he have a little girl in tow? Alfred dotes on that grandchild of his, as I'm sure you noticed. He would do anything for her. The Dorchesters know how to pamper their women." *Sometimes a little too much.* Sabrina, who was accustomed to having her own way, had not appreciated being sent home.

He straddled one of the stools at the counter much as he might swing his leg over the back of a horse, in no hurry to leave the kitchen. "My father and Alfred have been close friends for years. Since Dad doesn't have any grandchildren of his own, he's grandparenting vicariously through Alfred."

"No grandchildren?" Marlo sounded surprised. He didn't blame her. A house this size should have a covey of them. He'd thought it many times himself, in fact. But he needed a wife for that, and so far he'd effectively eluded matrimony, despite everyone's hopes to the contrary.

"I'm an only child," Jake assured her. "I can guarantee it." He enjoyed seeing a pink flush spread across those high, finely shaped cheekbones, but didn't give her time to be embarrassed. "Is there anything I can do to help you clean up? If you have any crates or boxes you'd like me to carry…"

He liked the way her eyes lit at the offer, even though she promptly refused his help. She was independent, that was obvious, but still seemed to appreciate being treated like a lady.

Jake felt an unexpected reluctance to leave the kitchen. These women had made it feel cozy and inviting. It took a special sort of magic that didn't often happen in his home. It was too big and the staff too part-time for it to ever become more than a lavish hotel of sorts, luxurious, comfortable and rather sterile. It was the kind of house good for entertaining large groups of people, which he did often, so it served its purpose well. Still, Jake would have preferred a home that was comfy and welcoming, the way the kitchen felt tonight. Not only that, it was a relief to escape the one-up-manship that often happened in crowds of wealthy people. He had grown tired of hearing about the latest cruise or land acquisition or jewelry purchase.

Out of the corner of his eye, he noticed the tall, dark-haired one staring at him as if his presence were slightly disconcerting. Her vivid blue eyes were curious and her short cropped hair was standing on end as if she'd been pulling at its tips. Apparently, caterers were usually left alone to clear up their messes.

"Thoughtful," he thought her heard her mutter under her breath but he wasn't sure. "Check." To him, she said, "It's what you pay for—not having to tote or carry." She flushed to the roots of her hair before adding, "You'd better be careful, offering to help us carry crates of dirty goblets. That's as appealing to us as it would be to tell your wife she needs to gain a few pounds because there would be more of her to love."

Jake felt laughter bubble in his throat. Beautiful, quirky and unexpected. Nice.

"Coffee then? I make a mean espresso, and my lattes are pretty good, too."

The woman seemed to enjoy talking to herself. She muttered something about being hospitable before saying in a louder voice, "Thanks, but no. We don't normally…"

"But I insist." He enjoyed watching Marlo's open, expressive face. Every thought and emotion she had seemed to pass across her features. It was easy to see what was on her mind without her uttering a word. And she appeared to be thinking he was an eccentric millionaire, emphasis on eccentric, for wanting to spend time with the caterer.

She clasped her hands in front of her, not knowing what to do with them. Guileless and transparent, she showed her nervousness. That, too, was in her favor, Jake thought. He liked a woman who didn't put on airs—one like Bette.

"We'd love to," Lucy answered for both of them. "There's plenty of coffee still hot." And when she thought he wasn't looking, she made a face at Marlo, as if to say, "What are our chances of ever doing *this* again?"

"Come into the library. It's more comfortable." He removed three hefty mugs from a cupboard, poured coffee and put them on a wooden serving tray while Lucy picked up what was left of the minicheesecakes. He indicated that Marlo should go first, as they made their way through the house toward a large, closed, wood-paneled door.

He watched her as she walked. *Long, shapely legs, a straight back, head held high...she'd be a natural in the saddle,* Jake deduced. He could imagine her on a filly that was fifteen-and-a-half or sixteen-hands high, or perhaps an even bigger horse.

The foyer through which they walked was larger than some entire houses, Jake thought, as their footsteps tapped against the marble floor. A richly carved table, weighed down with an enormous vase of fresh flowers, filled the center of the circular room from which doors led into other parts of the house. A vast staircase spiraled upward. Jake rarely noticed the luxury in which he lived, but imagining it through the lovely caterer's eyes, he wondered if it appeared pretentious, extravagant and over the top.

He led them into the library which was behind the first closed door. The door opened onto a vignette of ox blood–leather wing chairs, ottomans, a lavish area rug that covered most of the cherrywood floor. A gas fireplace burned brightly in the dimness in the room. Leather-bound books marched in neat rows down the shelves, collectors' items, mostly. The only ones that really got used were a basket of Bibles and history books. The others he never picked up. Artfully arranged on the shelves were carvings of horses, interspersed with Hammond family photos.

Normally, he didn't pay any attention to those photos, but tonight he realized that Sabrina had made her way into several of them, usually cuddling so close to him she could have been a second skin. In a closed glass case along one wall were dozens of gleaming trophies, decorated, again, with horses.

"I've been transported to a movie set," Marlo blurted, as she gazed around the room with huge eyes, her pink mouth puckered into a little bow of astonishment.

"Glad you like it." He put the tray onto a vast ottoman, gestured for them to sit down. "I want to personally thank you. The guests raved about the food. I gave your cards to several individuals. I'm sure you'll be getting calls. This crowd loves to entertain."

"And just what kind of 'crowd' is that?" Marlo asked.

He smiled at her. "A horsey crowd. Clients. Friends of the family. The people my father and grandfather deal with. Studs, you know."

Marlo's eyes grew wide. "I didn't notice *that* many good-looking, younger men in that group. Ow!" Then she glared at Lucy, who'd kicked her in the ankle.

Hammond spewed coffee back into his cup and burst out laughing. "Not *that* kind of stud. The horse kind. Stallions, standing at stud. My father and grandfather have owned a lot of good mares over the years. That's how Hammond Stables got started—with brood mares, very expensive ones, and valuable stallions. We're breeders. A lot of prizewinners have come out of our barn."

Marlo's face grew so red that Jake thought it might ignite. She didn't burst into flames but it was obviously a very close call. Jake realized that he liked a woman who blushed.

* * *

Dying on the spot would have been useful for hiding her embarrassment but Marlo couldn't manage it, here in gorgeous Jake Hammond's library. She considered crawling under the rug but decided tough it out. Fortunately, the man was obviously a well-bred gentleman who didn't make a big deal of her blunder.

Marlo liked that. In fact, there weren't many things about Jake Hammond that she *didn't* like. He came eerily close to fulfilling the requirements of her youthful list of romantic qualifications. Too bad he was already taken. By what she had deduced, Sabrina, Randall and Alfred already considered the union a done deal.

It was just as well. She was a poor match for the wealthy, refined man before her.

Lucy filled in the conversational gaps while Marlo gathered her wits about her again. They were talking about training horses when she finally felt confident enough to enter the discussion.

"It's something I enjoy, but I don't have enough time in my day to be as active as I'd like," Jake was saying. "I prefer working with the animals, but the buyers come first. Without them, we'd have no reason to raise horses in the first place."

"How did you learn to do it?" Marlo asked.

"From my grandfather. I was attached to his side like a tick to a dog when I was young. And what he didn't teach me, my father did. The Hammond family has been raising horses for generations, so maybe I learned by osmosis." He smiled and his eyes did that thing again that made Marlo's heart flutter. She almost wished he'd quit doing whatever it was that was making her have this reaction. No one like Jake would be interested in a girl like her.

Lucy gave a mouselike squeak as she looked at her watch. "Marlo, I have to get home. I promised I'd call my brother tonight, and it's getting late, even on the West Coast."

"You are welcome to use the phone in the library."

"I'm supposed to give him some phone numbers and addresses that I have on my computer at home. I'd better get going."

Marlo started to rise from her chair but Lucy waved her back. "No use both of us leaving."

"But we drove together," Marlo protested.

"I can call Marlo a cab," Jake offered, "if you need to leave in a hurry."

"Good idea. Thanks so much. Marlo, honey, call me in the morning." Without so much as a goodbye, Lucy shot out of the library. In moments, they heard the van fire up and pull away.

Marlo wanted to strangle Lucy with her bare hands, she decided, as her means of escape roared away. She knew exactly what Lucy was doing—giving her extra time with Jake, because she assumed he was a perfect fit for the List. Well, it wasn't going to work. The List indicated that the ideal man should "earn a good living" not be preposterously wealthy. She didn't know how to relate to people with money like that, even though he made it easier than she'd expected.

"More coffee?" Jake bent near her, carafe in hand. She smelled the woodsy cologne he wore and saw the fine weave of the arm of his jacket.

"I'd better not. I won't sleep all night." Not that she would, anyway, after this heady experience. She turned her eyes up toward his and became conscious of how close he was. "I have to apologize for my friend."

He stepped back, poured himself another cup and sat down. "Why?"

"Because those 'names and numbers' she had to give her brother were probably fictional."

He cocked his head to one side and a lock of dark hair fell over his forehead. Couldn't the man be unattractive from any angle at all?

"Lucy is playing matchmaker. I hope you'll excuse her. Sometimes she just doesn't think things through. Now, if you'll call me a cab…"

"Matchmaker?" He sounded amused, even pleased. To Marlo's amazement, he didn't appear to think the idea was ludicrous, just entertaining. She supposed that was a compliment, but it didn't undo her friend's machinations. Maybe she wouldn't wait until morning to throttle Lucy; perhaps she should stop at her house on the way home.

"Besides, there's no hurry. Where do you live?"

Marlo gave him the address.

"It's not far. I'll take you home myself."

"Oh, I couldn't… A cab is fine…really."

"Sure you could." He pulled off his jacket and rolled up his shirtsleeves as if he were about to go to work. His forearms were tanned and muscular. He wasn't a stranger to physical work, Marlo noted. "I've had enough coffee now to keep me awake until the New Year. No use taking a cab and wasting my alertness." He looked so appealing, so boyish and sincere that he was virtually irresistible.

Everything seemed to make worse the tumble of emotions coursing through her. Then why did she feel such an unwelcome attraction to Jake?

"I'm dying of embarrassment, you know. I don't want you to bother."

"No need. I'll enjoy getting out for a drive." He picked up the plate of cheesecakes. "Now that you know you're going home soon, do you want to have one of these?"

Marlo's stomach growled a response. She clamped a hand over her belly but it was too late. Hammond had heard it.

"I thought so. You were too busy to put any food in your own mouth."

"That's a little like stealing," Marlo pointed out. "It's your food. You bought it."

"Then help me eat it." He sank back into the leather chair in which he'd been sitting. Framed in dark leather and the faultless white of his shirt, he could have been posing for one of the handsome portraits that lined the staircase gallery.

Oh, why not? Marlo told herself. This was a once-in-a-lifetime moment. What was more, she knew just how good the Divas' cheesecakes were.

"Even my father said your food was an enormous hit at the party."

"'Even' your father?"

"His approval doesn't come easily." He paused a long time before adding, "Life has made him a suspicious man. When you get a compliment from him you can assume you've neared perfection."

"I'm flattered." *And delighted, overwhelmed, ecstatic and probably falling in love with you,* she might have added if she were being completely truthful. Of course, some things were better left unsaid.

"He's requested that I put you on notice. Hammond Stables will be doing a significant number of events this fall and we'd like you to cater all of them."

"As soon as the dates are fixed, I'll put them on our calendar." She should have left then but a comfortable languor washed over her. Jake seemed to feel it, too, and they sat in each other's presence silently for a long while. Finally, she placed her hands on the arms of the chair and pushed herself up. "Now, I'd better be going."

He stood swiftly. "Let me help you." He reached out to help her up. She felt his warm, slightly rough palm, calloused from the chafing of the reins, no doubt, and the gentle squeeze of his fingers that brought her to her feet.

Gentlemanly. Check.

Jake led her toward the garage, another massive space with a black-and-white tiled floor and a bank of lockers against one wall. He chose one of the four cars there, a black BMW.

Even his car fit the List! Marlo ran a hand across the soft leather seat before putting her right hand to her left forearm. She gave herself a pinch. It hurt. She wasn't dreaming.

It was easy to be silent, relaxing against the smooth leather, hearing the powerful drone of the engine, watching city lights go by. She sneaked a peek from the corner of her eye at her driver, his strong profile lit by streetlights and the glow from the dashboard. Marlo rued the fact that his lifestyle and his wealth were so foreign to her. She would have little idea how to live in his world, or he in hers.

Or maybe, she told herself, she was making unfair assumptions about Jake.

"Jake, what is it you want to accomplish with Hammond Stables?"

He turned and looked at her sharply. "What do you mean?"

Feeling as if she'd been x-rayed by lasers, she was glad when his eyes returned to the road. "Objectives, aspirations, wishes. Everyone who is successful has them."

"You're a funny little thing, you know that?"

At five feet nine inches, she was rarely called *little,* so she decided to take it as a compliment. "Why, thank you."

He threw back his head and laughed, and her heart skipped a beat at the sound. "You took me off guard. I believe you have a knack for that." He pressed his lips together to ponder the question. "Objectives, aspirations and wishes, huh? My objective is to continue the family business and take it to the next level, to raise the bar even further. My father and grandfather have done amazingly well and I feel it's my duty to continue the tradition.

I've already got my business plan in order." He looked at her again and his eyes twinkled. "Would you like to see it?"

"No, thank you." Marlo suddenly felt shy and prim, responses that were rare in her emotional vocabulary. "I was just making conversation. I didn't expect you to write a treatise or anything."

"It's okay. I happen to like something more than casual conversation. I enjoy meaty topics. If you really want to know, my personal aspiration is to someday settle down, get married and have those grandchildren my father thinks he's never going to get. Until then, I'm going to work at making my architectural firm one of the top in the city, and Hammond Farms recognized nationally."

He pulled into the driveway of Marlo's immaculate South Minneapolis bungalow. The darkness of the car's interior felt uncomfortably intimate. To her surprise, Jake lifted her hand from her lap to his lips and kissed it. "And the wishes will have to wait for later." He paused before continuing. "I overheard you and your partner talking back at the house. You said something that stuck with me. I wanted to know if you meant it."

They had said a *lot* of things. That would teach her to keep her mouth shut while she was working. The easy, breezy conversation she and Lucy maintained was usually just mindless chatter—emphasis on *mindless*. What part of their empty-headed banter had he overheard? Hopefully he *hadn't* heard them discussing the Cinderella List.

"You were discussing yourselves as children, as I recall," Jake prodded. Marlo paged through her memory bank. She had no idea that Jake, on his trips in and out of the kitchen, had overheard them.

"I heard you say that you had a lot of compassion for children who struggled to learn, and that you wished you knew a way that you could help to make a difference for them."

"I was a difficult child myself, according to my mother—at least until my parents discovered I was dyslexic. I transposed words and letters. My reading problems were mostly from seeing things backward." Marlo smiled ruefully. "Even though I overcame it quickly in academics, my mother says it didn't shake my penchant for doing other things in reverse order."

She'd always believed that her dyslexia and proclivity to come at things from the wrong end had deepened the compassion she felt for her nephew, Brady.

"I thought you might be interested in something I'm doing at the stables…if my father doesn't sink it before it starts." Jake's expression was cautiously neutral, as if he didn't want Marlo to guess what he was thinking.

He chose his next words carefully. "The changes I'm currently making at the stable have my father and me at odds. He's the opposite of calm and laid-back. He accuses me of being too easygoing and willing to go with the flow." His eyes crinkled and a slow smile graced his lips. "I like to think I'm a lover, not a fighter, but my father is not always amused."

"He doesn't trust you?"

"The only person my father has ever accepted unconditionally is his friend Alfred. They were boys together, best friends. My father calls Alfred's judgment 'impeccable.'"

"What awful things are you doing? Insisting the horses have weekly pedicures? Wear diamond-encrusted saddles? Eat gourmet oats?"

Jake's smile flashed in the dimness. "The show animals are practically doing that already—they have polished hooves, saddles and tack with bling, and highly regulated diets. That's not the problem."

"Then what is?"

"I'm starting a hippotherapy program at Hammond Stables. Dad calls it a wild idea, a notion that I'll lose interest in as soon as I find a high-rise to design.

"The program is designed for kids with special needs. And kids like you were—struggling with things beyond their control. Things like cerebral palsy, severe injury, mental and physical issues, strokes."

Compassionate. Marlo liked that in a man. *Check.* "And your father disapproves of…what exactly?"

"Dad doesn't feel disabled kids add to the 'ambiance' of the operation." Jake's expressive eyes darkened with anger. "He's afraid potential buyers might not like competing with children for time in the arena."

"What will you do?" she asked, feeling sympathy for his predicament.

"Ignore his protests for the time being. He hasn't forbidden it entirely—yet. I plan to start small, but to try to grow it quickly. I'm looking for compassionate volunteers who are willing to help with the program. People who can withstand my father's negativity."

"And you think I can?" Marlo was surprised. "Although I adored them as a child, I don't know a thing about horses. Not real ones. I fantasized about them, but the only ones I'm truly familiar with are of the *Black Beauty* and My Little Pony variety."

"That can be learned. What I'm looking for, Marlo, are people who *care.*"

She took a deep breath. Here she was, backing into something once again. Volunteering to work with horses when she'd never even ridden one. But one look at Jake, and she couldn't say no.

"When do we start?"

Chapter Three

Still giddy from the previous night, Marlo decided to stop at her sister's house for a cup of coffee before heading to work. When she swung into the driveway of the tidy white bungalow not far from her own, respect for Jenny and Mike, who had worked so hard to make this a safe, loving home for Brady, always surfaced.

No one who had not experienced it for themselves understood the struggle and pain that had transpired behind these windows with their blue shutters and yellow trim. Yet flowerboxes filled with a madcap assortment of red flowers, mostly geraniums, made the house look as though it belonged in a lighthearted film.

It was a good house in a pleasant older neighborhood, but Marlo knew that Jenny longed for something bigger, for her day-care children, but she and Mike chose to spend every extra penny they earned seeking help for Brady, who had been oxygen deprived at birth. Marlo didn't blame them. No one with a heart could resist Brady. He was certainly her own biggest weakness—he could reduce her to mush with one gleeful smile.

The day of his birth was still etched into her mind like carving in stone. A protective bond had formed between them that day that couldn't be broken. Marlo knew she'd do just about anything for her little nephew—especially anything that would make his life simpler and more enjoyable.

She rang the doorbell, opened the door and walked inside knowing that her sister had already been up for hours. The day care she ran opened at 6:00 a.m. for early arrivals.

"I'm in the kitchen," Jenny called. "You're just in time to help me cut sugar cookies."

Marlo kicked off her shoes—Jenny hated dirt on her carpet—and headed toward her sister's voice. Jenny was at the large island rolling a sheet of cookie dough. Cookie cutters in the shapes of bucking broncos, cowboy hats and a cowboy on a horse littered the area. The sweet aroma of vanilla permeated the kitchen.

"Hey, sis," Marlo greeted her. "How are you this morning? You look tired."

"I didn't sleep much last night. The little hamster wheels in there just wouldn't quit whirling. I kept thinking about my day-care kids and Brady."

Marlo looked out the door to see Jenny's day-care brood playing outside in the grass. They were laughing and running with red, blue and green balls, bouncing them off the ground and each other. Several had one hand in the air, swinging it in a circular motion. Brady, meanwhile, sat just outside the French doors to the deck, intently watching the other children.

"Why isn't Brady playing, too?"

"He's afraid." Jenny's chipper demeanor slipped a little. "He's okay when everyone is inside and I keep the din down to a dull roar, but the minute the kids go outside, he refuses to join them. It's progress to get him onto the deck."

"Why do you think that is?" Marlo asked calmly, suppressing the prick of sadness she felt at her sister's statement. She picked up a cutter and began to press out cookie shapes and lay them on baking sheets.

"He took a tumble and got a nasty scratch on his elbow last week and he's refused to have anything to do with the kids when they are running ever since."

Marlo stared out the window at the back of her small nephew. His slender neck and frail shoulders didn't look strong enough to hold the beautifully shaped blond head covered with baby-fine curls that always smelled of strawberry-scented shampoo. He appeared as fragile as the hummingbird currently dipping its beak into a nearby feeder. His white-blond hair and porcelain skin gave him the appearance of an otherworldly being, an angel, delicate and easily broken. It was no wonder, Marlo mused, that Jenny didn't push him to play with the other little rowdies on the grass.

Jenny wiped her hands on a towel and moved to stand by Marlo. "It breaks my heart," she said softly. "It's my fault he's not out there playing with those kids."

"Don't be a goose," Marlo said sternly. Even though she empathized deeply with her sister's pain, one of them had to remain clear-headed. "Of course it's not your fault. It's terribly unfortunate but the fact is that children can be injured in childbirth." Gently, she reached for her sister's hand. "No one blames you for Brady's issues."

"Well, they *should* blame me."

"Oh, Jen…" Marlo had prayed fervently that the unproductive guilt Jenny harbored be removed from her, but it was obviously not happening yet. What made it all the worse was Jenny's seeming inability to turn what had happened over to God. Instead, she continued to blame herself, never allowing the wound to heal.

"If I hadn't been so determined to tough out most of his labor at home, they might have known the umbilical cord was twisted and compressed. But no, not me. And look what it did to Brady."

Brady had been born oxygen deprived—hypoxia, Marlo thought they had called it—and the still, pale infant had been whisked away to a neonatal intensive care unit as soon as he was born. The result had been this beautiful, delicate boy with a lowered IQ, slowed language skills, poor balance and coordination and a marked inability to concentrate. Jenny had never forgiven herself. Marlo wished her sister would focus more on Brady's precious qualities—his loving personality, his perpetual good cheer, his sensitivity, the traits that made Brady who he was—and less on those other qualities.

"Babies are born in traffic jams, on kitchen tables and, in some countries, right in the fields. Childbirth is a natural process, Jenny, not an illness. How could you have known what was happening?"

"I'm his mother. I should have known."

Marlo's own chest tightened when her sister talked like this. "Forgive yourself and go on. God forgives us. If He can do that, then you should, too." After five years, Jenny still hadn't let go of her guilt and turned it over to God.

"Give the boy some credit for knowing himself, Jenny. He's not ready for roughhousing right now. Better he sit on the porch than get hurt." Marlo ground a cookie cutter hard into the soft dough. She hated sounding unsympathetic, but sometimes it was the only way to snap her sister out of this mood of blame.

"I don't want him to be a porch-sitter for the rest of his life!" Jenny dug for a tissue in her pocket, turned away and blew her nose.

When she turned back to Marlo, her cheeks were flushed. "You're right and I know it, sis, but sometimes…"

The damage to Brady's brain had left him with weak reasoning abilities and powers of logical thinking. Occasionally he was impulsive and unable to absorb the idea of consequences. Sometimes this worked in his favor, other times it did not, such as the time he'd decided to test what his mother meant by "hot" on the stove and came away with a second-degree burn on the palm of his hand. Other times he was abnormally cautious, like today.

His attention span was brief; he cried easily and was susceptible to perceived slights. But there were gifts, as well. Brady was exceedingly sensitive to people's emotions. More than once, when Marlo was feeling down, he'd given her a perceptive hug and a pat on the arm. "It's okay, Auntie Marlo," he'd say. Sensitive Brady could read and identify with another's hurt or pain, and yet he couldn't count past five.

"His irrational fears are getting worse," Jenny continued. "Next, we'll have an agoraphobic on our hands, as well."

"Aren't you the cheerful one today?" Marlo finished laying cookies on the baking sheet and put it into the oven. There was no point pursuing this line of conversation further, so she changed the subject. "I take it that this is cookie decorating day?"

"A cowboy theme. The kids outside are pretending to rope cattle." Jenny poured Marlo a cup of coffee and pointed to the kitchen table and chairs. "Sit."

They sat and Jenny stared into her cup a long time before continuing. "We can live with his disabilities, but not with his fear. The doctors say that someday he could hold a job, but not if he's afraid of every unexpected sound or movement."

"He's not six yet. He has time to learn." Perpetual optimism was another trait Marlo had learned from her aunt Tildy.

Even if she hadn't believed in Brady—and she did—she would never admit it to Jenny. Sometimes she felt as if she were propping up the entire family, and it was an exhausting endeavor.

"But *how?* And *when?*"

Brady, hearing the voices in the kitchen, left his perch on the deck and came inside. His pale, angelic features made Marlo want to scoop him into her arms and ward off the outside world that was so alarming to him. Instead she put out her hand for a high five. "Put 'er there, buddy. Wassup?"

Brady giggled. "You talk funny."

"Why aren't you playing with your friends?"

"Too hard."

"You mean they play too hard?"

He nodded fervently, his blond hair bouncing.

Marlo loved this little boy beyond words. She'd rocked him for hours on end when he was a newborn, allowing his exhausted parents to sleep. Marlo had patiently helped Brady learn to walk, while all Jenny could talk about was what might happen if he fell and hurt himself. Ultimately, she'd been the one to pry Brady from his mother's protective clutches long enough to pet the neighbor's dog, go down a slide and splash in the baby pool at the park. His life needed no detours.

"Come here and give your auntie Marlo a kiss, Brady boy. I've got to get to work." She tapped her cheek with her finger and, giggling, Brady complied.

"I love you, little buddy," Marlo whispered as Brady's soft breath skimmed her cheek. Brady threw his arms around her and hugged her tight.

"You're late," Lucy said when Marlo finally arrived at the Divas' kitchen. She was putting together leafy spinach salads with sliced hard-boiled eggs.

"I stopped at Jenny's for a cup of coffee."

"How is Brady doing? Last time I talked to your sister she said that she was afraid he might have strep throat."

"A false alarm, fortunately, but with him, she never knows." A wave of tenderness swept over Marlo. "The child never complains about anything."

Sometimes she wondered if she were being fair to Jenny by accusing her of being too cautious. Her sister simply couldn't resist being overprotective of her darling boy.

"Someone called for you this morning," Lucy said with studied nonchalance.

"Did you take a message?"

"I did not. I told him that if he wanted to talk to you he should show up here."

"It's not that health food distributor again, I hope. There's nothing like a reformed snack-food junkie to be a high-pressure salesman."

"No, not him. Better." Lucy's eyes sparkled with delight, giving rise to a suspicious foreboding in Marlo. Lucy was up to something.

"I don't have time to play around. Who called?" Before Lucy could answer, Marlo's eyes widened as Jake sauntered through their front door. Her heart did a traitorous flip. She willed herself to be calm.

"You can thank me later. Right now, I think I'll just slip into the storeroom and rearrange the supplies." With a wink, Lucy disappeared, leaving Marlo alone with the gorgeous Mr. Hammond. Marlo didn't know whether to pop Lucy in the nose or hug her.

"I brought your check." He tucked his hand into an inner pocket of his suit coat and pulled out a long white envelope.

"Thank you. I'm sorry you had to make a trip out of your way. You could have mailed it." She was, however, glad he hadn't. He was just as gorgeous as she remembered—and as sophisticated and charming, too. His smile was easy and his eyes intelligent-looking. She gave herself a little mental slap. What was she doing fantasizing about a client? She knew perfectly well what she was doing. She was comparing him to the List, and so far Hammond was a very good match. A very good match, indeed.

Chapter Four

"Are you sure you want to do this? Two devastating humiliations in one week might be too much for you." Lucy looked at Marlo with an expression that was half genuine concern and half repressed amusement. "We can postpone the Bridesmaids' Luncheon until you've recovered from your faux pas at the Hammonds' the other night."

Marlo turned an attractive shade of pink. "I must be thick as a brick to have blurted out what I did." Despite Jake's graciousness and avoidance of her error, thinking about it made her cringe. Studs...horses...what else?

"But he laughed, Marlo. He thought it was funny."

Sense of humor. Check. "Then he's a better man than I am."

"That goes without saying." Lucy turned around and the enormous sunflower-yellow bow on her backside almost brushed an entire row of swan-shaped cream puffs off the counter.

The annual Bridesmaids' Luncheon that Lucy and Marlo were hosting for their friends had started after Marlo had been asked to be a bridesmaid for the fourteenth time. It had begun half in jest and half because her friends had chosen the dresses with the deluded hope that they might be worn again. All had overlooked the fact that no dress ever worn by someone playing second fiddle to a woman in white lent itself to a second wearing.

Marlo had taken lemons and made lemonade by hosting this luncheon. She and Lucy required that everyone come in an old bridesmaid dress, and wear their hair in whatever fashion that particular bride had requested—an unflattering chignon or French twist, usually.

They served things like chicken Kiev on a bed of watery, undercooked wild and white rice, or minuscule medallions of beef on reconstituted mashed potatoes, duplicating typical wedding food as best they could. It wasn't truly authentic, however, since they refused to leave the meals on the counter until they'd cooled off before serving them.

Every year, when the guests began their yearly conversation about disbanding the Bridesmaids' Luncheon, Marlo would bring out the pièce de résistance, the item that brought them back year after year in their flouncy fashion disasters—the wedding cake. Few of her friends had tasted their own wedding cakes, other than for the obligatory shove-a-piece-into-each-other's-mouths photo. This year the cake was carrot cake, layered with melt-in-your-mouth vanilla cheesecake, cream cheese frosting, walnuts and slivers of grated carrots.

Lucy eyed Marlo critically. "Speaking of dresses, you haven't changed yet. Let me handle the kitchen. It's not that hard to scorch one pan of food and undercook another. Do you think the carrots have been boiling long enough? Is there any color left in them?"

Lucy edged Marlo toward the bedroom, where an array of fashion disasters awaited. "You should wear the pink tulle you wore to your sister's wedding," Lucy advised. "It enhances your skin."

"It makes me look like a gob of cotton candy."

"There are worse things. I have a dress that makes me look like an Eskimo Pie."

Marlo dropped onto the edge of the bed. "At least we've been able to go through most of these wedding traumas together. You're a good friend, Lucy. I don't tell you how much I appreciate you nearly often enough."

"I'm guilty of that, as well. You are the most loyal, supportive, enthusiastic person I've ever known. I hope you find that Prince Charming you are looking for, Marlo. You deserve it." Then Lucy glanced at the clock. "You'd better get ready. The doorbell is going to ring in five minutes.

"By the way, did you find a present to swap?"

Marlo regretted ever starting the regifting portion of the party. She was running out of things in her house as useless as her bridesmaid dresses.

"I have a set of knives that probably can't cut through air. It's the best I can do since I don't have any wedding gifts I want to get rid of." Marlo leaned heavily against the doorjamb. "It's getting more and more difficult to ignore the fact that I'm one of the last single women in the group."

"Whatdayamean? I'm single," Lucy protested.

"You don't count. Your man is doing a tour of duty overseas."

"Don't forget Angela, our beloved professional woman, control freak, neatnik and germaphobe." Lucy wrinkled her nose. "No man in his right mind would tangle with Angela."

Marlo didn't want to admit it to Lucy, but misery does, indeed, love company. Instead she headed toward her bedroom, took the pink confection out of her closet and put it on. Jenny had desired a Cinderella wedding, handsome prince and all. Unfortunately her brother-in-law, Mike, had looked more like a miserable, depressed marshmallow than a prince, in his white tuxedo.

An errant thought popped into her mind. What would Jake

Hammond look like in a groom's white tuxedo? He'd carry it off, no doubt, just like he seemed to do with everything else. That, she realized, was something she should not dwell on, and she hurried to put on her makeup.

Marlo was barely dressed when she heard a commotion at her front door. Three women in billowing skirts were trying to break in. Tiffany came through first, in black tulle, looking as gloomy as if a funeral dirge were droning in the background. Jenny flitted in next, wearing a burgundy sheath with black lace inserts in the front and back, which made her look as if she was wearing a nightgown. She stood on tiptoes and gave Marlo a peck on the cheek. "You look stunning as always, sis."

After Jenny, Linda arrived in a diaphanous chiffon number and Becky in royal blue. Christine, looking sour, refused to remove her jacket to show everyone what was underneath, citing ten extra pounds and several safety pins holding the dress together. Angela in Kermit green looked as tart as a lime.

"More proof that Angie will never find a man who can tolerate her," Lucy whispered to Marlo, and received a poke in her ribs for the effort.

The Bridesmaid Club had arrived in full force.

"How's your love life, Marlo?" Linda inquired over the last of her chicken Kiev.

This was the moment Marlo had been dreading—more so this year than others. Inevitably, when the luncheon conversation waned, her love life became the topic of choice. Her friends' favorite activity was living vicariously through her dates. After a few years of marriage, they were beginning to view dating as a blast from the past and wanted to be reminded of how wonderfully romantic it was. They'd obviously forgotten the actual realities of dating—being fixed up, stood up or waiting by a phone that didn't ring. In Marlo's experience, dating could only be romanticized in hindsight.

Before Marlo got her mouth open to say as much, Lucy unexpectedly took the stage and blurted, "Marlo has met someone interesting." Every head turned in Marlo's direction.

"Does he fit the Cinderella List?" Jenny blurted.

Marlo nudged her ankle, not wanting Jenny to discuss their childhood game. Even louder, Jenny said, "I didn't know your ideal man actually existed, Marlo."

"List? What list?" Becky pounced on Jenny's words. "An 'ideal' man actually exists? And you've found him, Marlo? Have you been holding out on us?"

"I think that's absolutely wonderful!" Until that moment, Angela had been unusually quiet. Everyone turned to stare at her. Angela was a lot of things, but gracious wasn't usually one of them. Angela's features flushed with happiness. "I'm overjoyed, Marlo. It makes everything even more perfect."

The group was taken aback by the transformation. Angela *never* beamed. She waited a beat before announcing, "I'm getting married!" The room was silent, as the astonishing news sank in, then everyone erupted in a cacophony of happy chatter.

The news hit Marlo like a piano dropped off a ten-story building. *Angela* married? Angela *married?* Bossy, controlling, frenzied and career-oriented Angela who had never had a nice thing to say about any man she'd ever dated? *She* was getting married?

Now Marlo was the only single woman in the Bridesmaid Club and was surprised to realize that she actually cared that she was losing this elusive race. She'd fallen behind in an unspoken marriage competition she hadn't even meant to join. She felt an unexpected twinge of longing. Even more confusing were the images of Jake Hammond that skittered through her mind…the

broad shoulders, a flashing white smile turned her way, his sur-
reptitious peanut butter sandwiches with Bette….

Then a more practical thought came to her: if Angela got
married, it meant another wedding—with cake and flowers and
bridesmaids—and another dress. Fortunately or unfortunately,
the Bridesmaid Club would survive and thrive another year.

Chapter Five

Marlo's head swirled with disbelief as the rest of the ersatz bridesmaids continued chattering and squealing with joy.

She hadn't realized until this moment how much she'd counted on Angela to be part of the single contingency in this group of married friends. Feeling like the Lone Ranger minus Tonto, Marlo painted a stiff smile on her face. She refused to rain on Angela's parade.

"He's perfect for me," Angela babbled, in a very un-Angela-like way. "So forceful and smart. He's the CEO of a manufacturing firm." She looked doe-eyed and utterly smitten. "I've always loved men who can take charge. My knees feel weak when I'm around him."

A little like hers, Marlo thought, when Jake Hammond has smiled at her. She'd had no idea until that moment just how vulnerable she was to his charm.

"It's a good thing you met someone, Marlo, since you are now the only officially single woman in our group," Becky pointed out unhelpfully. "Who'd have thought?"

No one, apparently. They all appeared rather stunned, like

victims of an emotional hit-and-run. Several pairs of eyes fixed on Marlo, shining sympathy in her direction. For a bunch of women who in their college years had pronounced men "unnecessary," they'd certainly come full circle. And Lucy's announcement had underscored the fact that Marlo was now the group mascot—single and obviously pitiable.

"Marlo, you are a sly fox. If it weren't for Lucy, we wouldn't have heard about him at all!" Linda waggled a finger at her. "Knowing the kinds of parties you cater, he must be a big deal, fancy-schmansy, right?"

They drummed questions at her like hail on a tin roof, until she couldn't tolerate another word. She held up her hands to silence them. "This is Angela's day. Let's not talk about me. Cake, anyone?"

No one noticed when Marlo slipped into the kitchen, where she stood with the heels of her hands braced against the tiled counter, eyes closed, praying frantically that she would allow nothing—including jealousy, envy or resentment—to mar Angela's day.

By the time the women left in a swirl of chiffon, lace and satin, Marlo's head pounded like a kettledrum, spurred by memories of her own dashed wedding dreams. Even though she had no interest in Jeremiah anymore, the memories of her pain were vivid as a body blow.

Lucy expressed her friend's malady succinctly, as she and Jenny, who had remained behind to help, cleared the table and toted the dishes into the kitchen. "Stings, doesn't it, to have the practically unweddable Anglea get married before you do?"

"It does." Marlo sank onto a kitchen chair. "I've always believed I am independent and resourceful, not dependent or needy. If so, why do I feel like something is wrong with me?" Her memories drifted into that old morass of pain. "Not every man will be unfaithful like Jerry was, right? A good man just hasn't come along yet, that's all." There was nothing wrong with being single. She just didn't want to spend her life like that.

"What about the Cinderella List?" Jenny pointed out. "Does a man with your requirements even exist? Maybe you've set the standards too high."

"It was just a *game,* Jen…." Marlo wondered when it had turned into something more in her mind. She turned to glare at Lucy. "And what was that nonsense about Jake Hammond?"

"Purely diversionary. Just a little something for the piranhas to chew on."

Marlo didn't know whether to be angry or amused by the ridiculousness of it all.

Jenny slipped out of the room and returned some minutes later with her faux fur stole and a piece of folded white typing paper in her hand. "I'd better go, ladies. As usual, the Bridesmaids' Luncheon was a huge hit."

It had been a hit, so why did Marlo feel a fierce headache coming on?

"Here." Jenny thrust the piece of paper at Marlo. "I jotted this down. Maybe it will clarify things for you."

After Jenny was gone, Marlo walked into her bedroom and sat down on the bed to open the note her sister had given her. What was Jenny up to now?

Marlo,
Maybe this new guy will meet all your requirements…you deserve the very best.

    The Ideal Man, According to Marlo Mayfield
√ Handsome (dark hair preferred)
√ Good teeth, great smile
√ Well educated, intelligent

√ Emily Post manners (thoughtful, courteous, gracious,
   hospitable)
√ Earns a decent living
√ Sophisticated, charming, chivalrous
√ Looks good in jeans and suits
√ Appreciates fine food (and smells like oatmeal-raisin
   cookies)
√ Thoughtful, compassionate, intuitive
√ Sense of humor
√ Clever and willing to try new things, brave
√ Knows what the words *ebullient, anthropomorphize*
   and *hubris* mean
√ Health and disability insurance
√ 401K
√ Faith in God

Can love be far behind?
Love, Jenny

Marlo studied the List thoughtfully, her gaze falling on each
line and recalling many of the conversations she and Jenny had
had over the years. Her sister's memory was good—in her hur-
riedly written note, she hadn't missed a single quality required
of Marlo's current-day Prince Charming. The silly childhood
game had somehow managed to grow up right with her.

Angela's unexpected announcement had only underscored
her single state. It had also brought up her time with Jerry and
her own thwarted wedding. The pain might be gone, but the
promise she'd made to herself remained. Never would she do to
another woman what the "other woman" had done to her.

After a couple of restless hours, Marlo did the only thing she
knew would keep her mind off the ridiculous games her mind

was playing with itself. She baked. There was nothing more therapeutic than kneading bread dough.

It's the twenty-first century, she mused, as she thumped a fist into the risen dough and felt the soft resistance against her knuckles. *Women don't need a man to be complete.* She punched the doughy mass again. What were her friends thinking?

She already knew the answer to that question. They were thinking that because they were content in their marriages, they wanted her to be happy, too. The teasing had all been in good fun. It was just too bad she wasn't having any.

It was the Lord who planned her days and hours, and Marlo wanted to listen to Him, not her changeable emotions. Doing that when she'd met Jeremiah was the biggest mistake of her life. When—if—she did meet someone, Marlo prayed that God would make it clear that she wasn't treading on someone else's territory.

While the bread was in the oven, she whipped up a batch of cookies, took a shower, put extra-strength gel in her hair and pulled it into rebellious spikes. Then she slipped into a T-shirt and bib overall shorts. Looking all of sixteen years old, she padded barefoot downstairs to remove the bread from the oven and bake the last of the cookies.

She flinched when the doorbell rang. Surely Angela hadn't come back to rub more salt in her wounds. That would be just her luck.

Jake Hammond stood on her top step looking debonair and perfectly at home, holding a silver serving tray and a whisk. Jake was probably the only man in the world who could make kitchen utensils look inordinately masculine in his hands. A small shiver went up her spine. Excitement? No, she told herself, she was simply chilly.

"What are you doing…?" Then she remembered her manners. "How nice to see you, Mr. Hammond. Can I help you?"

"I found these things in my kitchen. I tried to drop them off at Dining with Divas, but the shop was closed. I hope you don't mind that I brought them here. I thought perhaps you'd need them soon." Her mind locked at the idea of him going to such effort when a telephone call would have sufficed.

"W-would you like to come in?" Marlo stammered finally, overtaken by a host of conflicting emotions. The man was holding a whisk, she reminded herself, not a bouquet of roses. Handsome, great smile, good manners, thoughtful… Items on the List swirled in her brain.

"Don't mind if I do." He sauntered into her house and it suddenly felt crowded, as if he'd taken all the space and air it had to offer. Jake's obvious athleticism was apparent beneath khaki trousers, and a caramel-colored polo shirt did something rather spellbinding to his eyes. "It smells awfully good in here."

His gaze traveled around the room, a place that could only be described as a foodie's residence. There were poster-size prints of loaves of bread and decadent desserts like tiramisu, flan and strawberries with whipped cream. Placards that proclaimed dozens of ways to cook with chocolate hung in her living room like most people displayed family portraits. The elegant but genteelly worn furniture were beloved castoffs. It was as cozy, charming and idiosyncratic as he'd expected.

"I'm making bread and cookies. Would you like some?" she asked politely, as if it was the least she could do. The timer sounded on her stove. "There are the cookies now."

"Absolutely." The invitation delighted him. "Do you know how long it's been since I've had homemade bread?"

"It was on Saturday actually. With the bruschetta we served."

"Homemade in an actual home, then. When I was a little boy, my grandmother baked a lot. Now she and my grandfather travel most of the time, doing touch-and-goes out of the ranch. My mother thinks too much time in the kitchen is beneath her." He missed the homey, domestic woman she'd once been. Now she was a world-hopping, Nordic-walking vegetarian. For a man who liked comfortable, homely things, it had been a big adjustment. Being good in the kitchen was an *upward* status symbol in his mind. The triumph of the stables was wonderful, but he often wondered if his parents lost themselves somewhere in that success.

He moved through the house, stopping to study the contemporary-looking line drawings framed over her fireplace, charmed by the quirky, eclectic mix. "These are unusual."

"My nephew drew those when he was three. Unfortunately, Brady's attention span is brief. Five minutes at something is an eon to my nephew."

Jake noted that she sounded wistful, especially when she added, "I always want to see potential in those childish sketches, because Brady has a lot of challenges to overcome. I have dozens of uncompleted drawings, so I decided to frame a few. You'd be surprised how many people comment on my taste in modern art."

"And savvy, too." He didn't try to hide his amusement. "Usually, you have to pay big money for things that look like this." The smile that spread across her face brought her back from some dark thoughts he didn't understand. She was beautiful when she smiled.

He paused at the bookcase which divided the living room from the dining area. On the living-room side were books that revealed Marlo's eclectic interests. Bibles and devotionals, deep-sea diving and mountain climbing, Chihuahuas and Great Danes, the classics and comic strips, South American authors and the North Pole—hints, no doubt, at her paradoxical personality.

The other side of the bookcase revealed an entirely different side of Marlo, he observed. If she didn't have every cookbook every published, she was well on her way. James Beard and Julia Child rested comfortably with *Birthday Cakes for Toddlers, Salsa Extravaganza* and *Sushi for the Timid.*

"You can tell a lot about a person by the types of books they own," Jake commented, as he sidled toward the kitchen counter and slid onto a tall stool. Marlo trailed after him and automatically poured him a mug of coffee.

"What do my books say about me?"

"For one thing, you are very spiritual. I also gather that you are diverse, eclectic and interested in a wide variety of subjects." She was complex. Jake liked that in a woman.

"At least you didn't tell me I'm a confused mess. After this day, that's certainly how I feel. I had friends here for a luncheon, and it didn't turn out quite as planned." Jake watched her face. It was obvious that she thought she'd said too much, and she clamped her lips together, as if to prevent another extemporaneous word from slipping out. He left the statement alone, instinctively knowing something important had happened, and sensing that she didn't want to talk about it. Deftly, she changed topics. "I apologize about the whisk. I would have come over to pick it up."

As Jake studied her, she put her hand over her heart as if to protect herself from his gaze. She was as uneasy as a new colt that had not been handled properly, shy and jumpy but no less adorable. Jake's curiosity—and interest—grew.

"That's not the only reason I came. I wanted to know if you'd thought any more about what we discussed the other night. I wanted to give you a little time, in case you wanted to reconsider your answer."

"That's nice of you, but I'll be there at the hippotherapy program. I keep my word. Besides, it's a chance for me to see what it's all about. I want to see what it does for the children. Maybe my nephew would benefit from it."

"A woman who keeps her promises. I like that." The more he learned about this woman, the more he liked what he knew.

Chapter Six

Waking up from a delicious dream about Jake Hammond, Marlo opened one eye, stared at the ringing telephone and willed it to be quiet. Regretting that she'd turned off her answering machine, she rolled over twice, enveloping herself in bedding like a tortilla wrap, wormed an arm free of the blankets and picked up the phone. "This is Marlo's answering machine," she growled. "Marlo is sleeping. Call back later. No, call back on Monday. Late. Not before 7:00 p.m."

"You have a very strange message on your machine, Miss Mayfield," a silky, perfectly awake male voice responded. "Now be a good answering machine and go wake up your owner."

Her eyes popped open wide, sleep banished. "Very funny," she groaned. "Haven't you heard of Saturday? Sleeping in? A day off?"

"All highly overrated. Especially on a beautiful day like this. Would you like to meet my horses today?"

"Really? You mean it?" She flipped back across the bed, unwrapping herself.

"The hippotherapy program will be up and running soon. I'd like to show you what I have planned." Jake's voice was as tempting as the Pied Piper's tune.

No sales pitch needed here, Marlo thought. The man could melt her with a sentence. Besides, if it could help kids like Brady, she was all over it. But there was no need to look overeager, either. He didn't need to know just how much she enjoyed being in his presence.

"Frankly, I'm flying under the radar right now," he continued. "If the program is in place before my father realizes the extent of it, he may just leave it alone."

"And if he doesn't?"

"I'll cross that bridge when I come to it." Jake seemed to formulate his words carefully. "I have an equal share in the business, so Dad's voting power is no more or less than mine, but I'd rather not have to remind him of that."

Marlo's impression of Randall Hammond was one of a determined, unbending, intimidating personality with a military air and manner, an inflexible man who probably wouldn't accept a setback or defeat easily—even at the hands of his own son.

"I'll pick you up in thirty minutes. Wear something comfortable. We'll stop for breakfast on the way to the stables."

Before she could reply, he ended the conversation.

Wondering what she'd gotten herself into, she stretched like a tabby in the sun. Thirty minutes? She sat up, stuffed her bare feet into a pair of fuzzy, pink slippers and shuffled to the bathroom.

The phone was ringing again when she stepped out of the shower some minutes later. This time it was Lucy.

"I'm going shopping. Want to come with me?"

"Sorry. Another time." Marlo studied herself in the bathroom mirror as she talked. Her dark hair curled and spiked around her face and her cheeks were rosy from the heat of the shower. "I'm going to Hammond Stables for a tour."

"Whoa. He's smooth. And fast. He's invited you already?"

"He has an ulterior motive. He's racing to get his hippotherapy program up and running. Don't think for a moment that this is about me."

"How can you be so sure?"

"Hello? Did you notice how Sabrina hung all over him the other night? And how he didn't once brush her off? Besides, she told me she was planning a wedding," Marlo said, "and I don't doubt it for a moment. Even if the groom is a little reluctant, Sabrina will make it happen. There's no way on earth I'd get in the middle of that relationship. You know me better than that."

"Then why are you so willing to help him? I'd spend my energy on someone with marriage potential."

"Because life is about more than dating and mating. He's onto something with the horses. My motivation, truth be told, is Brady. I'll tell you about it later if you promise not to announce it all to the Bridesmaid Club."

"I want to know every detail. It almost makes me wish I weren't going shopping…*almost.*"

By the time Marlo had pulled on a pair of blue jeans, a white shirt and a woven leather belt, her doorbell was ringing. She grabbed a baby-blue, zippered sweatshirt out of a drawer and, lacking boots, slid her feet into tennis shoes and hurried to answer the door.

Jake was standing on the porch, looking as yummy as ever. Marlo was definitely in big trouble.

"You don't give a girl much chance to pretty up, do you?" Marlo accused, as she stepped onto the front porch and closed the door behind her.

Jake smiled, pleased with her natural appearance. Her hair was still damp and the only makeup she'd had time to apply was a bit of lipstick. She was utterly unconscious of how much simplicity became her. With her dark hair, long eyelashes and faintly tanned complexion, she was as naturally lovely as a woman could be. He approved. It was a delightful change from the high-heeled, blood-red, heavily made-up, high-powered female architects at his firm.

"I want to get to Franco's before the food is gone." He tucked her arm around his and she didn't resist. *A good sign,* he thought.

"I have plenty of food here. Want me to scramble some eggs?" She skipped to keep up with him as he strode down the sidewalk. "I also make a mean frittata."

"I know you can cook. You do it all the time." He smiled down at her from his six-foot-two height. "I'd like to give you a break."

He watched her nose wrinkle. "You don't like that idea?"

"Are you a mind reader or something?"

He laughed at her dismayed expression. "I work with horses every day. I'm always watching for subtle signs of what's going on with them. It's second nature now, I guess." He opened the door of his hybrid car and helped her in.

"I'm not sure if it's a compliment or not, to be as easy to read as a four-legged animal." Marlo buckled her seat belt and leaned back.

"I suppose that depends on how much the one doing the comparing likes horses," Jake said, as he slid behind the wheel. "When I compare a person to a horse, it is a major compliment for the human."

Mollified, Marlo settled into the seat. "Sorry. I don't mean to be unappreciative. It's just that because Lucy and I cook so much and are pretty good at it, it's hard to find a restaurant that genuinely surprises or pleases us. If we eat out it's at a sushi place or an Asian fusion spot, food we don't normally make ourselves. I don't mean to be a food snob, but usually I prefer my own food to eating out." She blushed prettily.

Jake liked a woman who blushed. It seemed rare these days. "Oh, ye of little faith," he chided. "I appreciate your honesty. But don't worry. You'll like this place, I promise."

"Franco's. I don't think I've heard of it."

"Good. Then it will be a surprise." Jack adeptly navigated an on-ramp to the freeway and took a deep, satisfying breath of fresh air.

It was easy to relax in her presence. There were no uncomfortable gaps and edges that were sometimes present with people who didn't know each other well. Being with Marlo felt natural, as though they were meant to spend time together. Jake was surprised at just how much he liked the idea.

Franco's was a narrow structure wedged between two gray-block warehouses. On the left was a long-term storage center, and on the right a furniture rental business with a pathetic brown-and-beige-plaid hide-a-bed, a chipped side table and a lamp with a tipped shade in the window.

"Somehow, I didn't expect this would be your kind of eatery." Marlo sat straighter in her seat and took notice.

"A working man's café. The best kind." He pulled into the single available parking place, slid the key from the ignition and turned to grin at her.

"Your eyes crinkle when you smile, you know," she said. Then, appearing to realize she'd been a little too candid, clapped her hand over her lips.

"Is that good or bad?" Jake found himself enjoying this.

"Sorry, I didn't mean to be so blunt. I just meant that you aren't much like your father, are you?" She frowned. "There I go, doing it again, putting my foot in my mouth. I only meant that you're very cheerful and easygoing. It was supposed to be a compliment."

"No offense taken."

He watched her closely as they walked into Franco's restaurant. It was a garish combination bistro and truck stop. The counter stools were filled with men wearing denim shirts and jeans. There was not a tie or a pair of wingtips in sight. Several men looked at Marlo with interest, and Jake found himself moving protectively near her. He took her hand, which felt warm and tiny in his. She didn't protest, so he moved a little closer. Skittish fillies required a good deal of patience.

Tacky artificial grapevines wound across the ceiling, down several cheap artificial pillars and circled the cash register. More important, the pastry case was filled with the most delectable-looking pastries Jake, at least, had ever seen.

"Franco used to cook on a cruise ship," he explained, seeing the bewildered expression on Marlo's face. "Just wait."

At that moment a small man with a bald head and fuzzy black mustache sailed out of the back carrying a pan of caramel rolls bright with the glistening sheen of a buttery caramel topping. He put the pan on the counter, dished up two plate-size rolls and presented them to Jake and Marlo with a flourish. She held the plate to her nose and breathed in the aroma. Jake was almost positive that he heard her murmur, "Exquisite, just like Chanel No. 5."

"Eggs, Jake? Rhubarb fritter, French toast? Steak?"

"Whatever you feel like, Franco. Today's special is fine. Just beware, my friend Marlo is a caterer, so she's hard to impress."

That, he realized later, was like waving a red flag in front of a bull.

Marlo was still eyeing the fresh-squeezed orange juice and fruit compote when one of the waitresses brought them a pile of sausages and bacon and a basket of still-warm-from-the-oven muffins.

"There are omelets coming, and Franco has a coffee cake he wants you to try," the woman informed them. "And save room for some caramel-walnut bread pudding. It's a new recipe, and he wants your opinion."

"I take back any concerns I might have had about eating out with you," Marlo told him between bites. "I'll do this with you anytime."

"Anytime?" He watched her eyes flicker with an unspoken emotion and noted that she hesitated—but only slightly—before answering.

"I guess not *anytime*. This place closes for the night, doesn't it?"

"It's a breakfast and lunch place. He usually closes about 3:00 p.m. unless there's something special going on." Jake put his hand on top of hers as it lay on the table. "I'm going to remember that, Marlo. Don't be surprised when I call."

"I have never eaten a breakfast as wonderful as this one," Marlo declared some time later, as she pushed herself away from the table.

And Jake had never experienced this kind of breakfast companion before. She'd approached every bite of food with a sense of anticipation and delight, savored each flavor on her tongue. He could have been eating with a food critic from the *New York Times*.

"I remember my first breakfast in Poland," Jake said, as he polished off a fat omelet filled with vegetables, along with a steak and hash browns. "You can imagine my surprise when the waiter brought me a Polish sausage with mustard and a hunk of bread and nothing else. My stomach churned all day as a result. That was years ago, of course."

"Do you travel a lot? My closest brush with Poland *is* the sausage."

"My firm does a lot of projects abroad, but I avoid them if I can. Ever since I had the idea about the hippotherapy program, my heart isn't in the travel." He waved a piece of crisp, golden bacon and Marlo surprised him by leaning forward to bite into it. He plucked a leftover sausage off her plate in retaliation.

"I grew up in a house of privilege. What I wanted, I got. Cars, horses, education, you name it. What I'd always taken for granted was beyond the dreams and expectations of most people. And some are born with even more significant strikes against them—kids with disabilities and physical issues, for example. I finally realized that I could no longer live with myself if I didn't give back some of what I've been blessed to have."

He flushed, wondering if he'd said too much. It was too easy to talk to this woman. "Sorry. I don't mean to bore you with my 'aha' moments about being a spoiled rich kid."

"Don't be sorry." She put her hand over his. "I only wish more people would have those moments." He could feel her light touch and the warmth of her fingers on his. Then Franco came by with a fresh pot of coffee. Jake was sorry when she pulled back away. Her touch was like the rest of her—light, ethereal, warm.

"How about you, Marlo? What drives you?"

He watched her put cream into her coffee and stir it thoughtfully. "My faith. My family. Doing what is right. How I am to follow Jesus." She blushed and looked at him, as if checking to see how he was taking this.

This was important to her, Jake knew. He leaned forward on his elbows and nodded encouragingly.

"I always felt a little defective, considering that I've always done things the hard way, like a salmon swimming upstream, until I realized that the Bible is full of backward examples."

"How so?" Though she seemed to expect it, he wasn't uncomfortable with Marlo's statement.

"God's famous for taking unlikely, unqualified people and using them for His purposes. He has people backing into their potential all the time. Look at Paul, for example. He persecuted the church. He was practically a terrorist, but he ultimately became a missionary and defender of the church. If there was hope for Paul, there certainly is for me."

"And look what happened to Peter, a simple fisherman."

"You *do* understand." Her expression brightened and grew more animated.

Jake felt like the proverbial moth being drawn to the flame.

"Jesus is all about love. It seemed to me that using my gift, my cooking ability, and running my business with the intent to serve and to bring joy—and to show love in my own unique way—was a good place to start. I want to be a first-class caterer of course, but I also want to be known as the caterer who cares." She paused. "'The caterer who cares.'" Marlo rolled the words across her tongue as if she tasted them. "Maybe that should have been our business logo."

"You don't need the logo. It shows anyway. I noticed immediately." For him, part of her charm, Jake knew, resided in her obvious faith.

The slash of dimple in his cheek winked as he smiled at her, and Marlo felt any reluctance she'd felt toward involving herself with this man soften. She was like butter on toast, her reservations quickly melting away.

"That man can work miracles with eggs. I'm gaining weight just thinking about the pastries!" she said, as she buckled herself into Jake's car.

"Glad you liked it," Jake said, sounding genuinely pleased.

She studied him, taking in his profile, the pleasant smile lines that crinkled around his eyes, and the tanned skin of an outdoorsman. "I have to admit, I was surprised by your choice. I thought r—" She clamped lips shut. She'd almost said "rich men."

"It's below me, you mean?" Much to his credit, he didn't look insulted, only amused.

"I'm sorry. My brain is in carb overload and it's made me stupid. No offense meant."

"None taken. I spend a lot of my day dealing with people with too much money and too much time on their hands. Franco's is my way of reminding me who the real population is."

"What do you mean?"

He shrugged lightly. "People who are trying to decide if six bathrooms in their house is enough or if they should have seven, for example. Sometimes it's hard to take when a good share of the world's population doesn't even have a roof overhead."

Her curiosity was piqued. "You're not what I expected you to be."

"In what ways?"

"You're friendly, for one. To a lot of our clients, Lucy and I are invisible. We're hired by an assistant, introduced to the house by a servant, and leave by the back way when the party is done. I don't mind, because it's part of the job. Frankly, I didn't expect to see you in the kitchen. What's more, you were very gracious and helpful."

"Blunt, aren't you?"

"I don't know any other way to be, I'm afraid. My family says I don't just put my foot in my mouth occasionally, but that it's my foot's default location. You've probably already noticed that I speak first and think later."

"I hope you'll like Hammond Stables." Amusement flickered in his dark eyes. "But if you don't, I can be sure you'll tell me."

"I'd like to know more about your program," Marlo admitted.

It didn't even occur to Marlo that involving herself in the program meant involving herself very closely with the man she was sitting next to, as well. She had no thought that she might be backing into something dangerous, something that might break her heart.

"Hippotherapy can be used in physical, occupational or speech therapy," Jake told her as they drove. "It is a treatment strategy that makes use of the movement of a horse. With hippotherapy, the horse influences the rider, not the other way around. The rider must respond to the horse, not vice versa." He turned to her as the city whizzed by and the landscape began to grow more and more rural. There were still houses everywhere, but on much larger parcels of land, and neighbors were farther apart.

"*Hippo* is the Greek word for *horse*," Jake continued. "I took a little Greek in undergraduate studies. I thought perhaps someday I would like to read something in its original text."

Intelligent and well read. Check.

"You mentioned having a nephew who might benefit from a riding program."

"I think I spoke out of turn," she admitted. "My sister and I don't always agree where Brady is concerned. It's difficult to explain."

Marlo had known from the moment Brady was born that she was to play a special role in his life. She was to speak for the normal little boy in Brady, the part of him that wanted to run and play, to get dirty and fall down and scrape his knee. She spoke for the part of Brady that Jenny refused to hear. How did one put that into words?

He heard something unsteady in her voice, and he turned to look at her. "It's okay. Tell me when and if you want."

It was virtually impossible, Marlo decided, to resist anyone who was persistently cheerful and easygoing as Jake. She felt a little more of herself melt inside, like chocolate softening in the sun.

This man is dangerous, a small voice inside her said. *It would be very easy to fall in love with him.* She pushed the preposterous notion out of her mind. *Taken,* she reminded herself. *He's taken.* Nothing was more important to her than that bit of information.

Chapter Seven

She hung on every word he said, Jake observed. He had an apt pupil in Marlo, no doubt about that. Not everyone—his father and Sabrina included—wanted to understand the nuances of his new project.

"Equine movement is variable and rhythmic. Staying on a horse requires balance, good posture and strength. When the horse changes gaits, the rider has to subtly adjust in order to stay astride. The movement affects posture, the senses, motor skills and so much more. Therapists tell me that no machine can duplicate the muscle movement of a horse—side to side, as well as up and down and forward and back." He glanced over to see if Marlo was still listening. She was. "It's remarkably similar to a human gait. Keeping balance on a moving horse strengthens the same muscle groups the kids would use to walk, sit or reach."

"I had no idea. I suppose I've never really thought about it before, but it makes sense with a child touching, smelling, feeling and hearing a horse. It would stimulate all the senses at once."

"Children who have never uttered a word have suddenly begun to say the names of their horses. Kids who have never been out of their wheelchairs get to see the world from a vantage point the rest of us take for granted, standing on our own two feet." Jake felt his excitement building just at the idea. "This is life-giving, Marlo."

"Well, you've certainly convinced me!" Marlo said, as the miles and minutes flew by on their way to the ranch. "How did you first get involved?"

"I had a friend in school with cerebral palsy. A lot of kids didn't want anything to do with him because of his disability, but Buddy was a great guy, smart and funny. We talked a lot about his frustrations and his wish to be like other kids. He was particularly fascinated with my family's business and with horses. I don't know how many times he told me he wished he could ride a horse. One day I said I'd help him do it."

"Just like that?"

"Teenage boys aren't always known for thinking through the possible consequences of their actions." He amazed himself sometimes, that he and the others had even dared to try. Fortunately, he'd developed a little more common sense over the year. "I'm not sure either of us thought about it much at all, we just did it.

"I roped in a couple of guys who worked with the horses to help us. We put a saddle on a gentle horse and hoisted Buddy onto its back. The three of us kept him balanced in the saddle and walked around the arena—out of the sight of my father, of course."

"Then what happened?" Her blue eyes were very wide, like Cammi's got when he was telling her a tall tale. "Did anyone get hurt?"

"No, fortunately. We just got him down again and I took him home. Our parents were never the wiser." Jake shook his head ruefully, still amazed that nothing serious had happened as a result. "We could have easily dumped Buddy on his head, but I doubt he would have minded."

"You were pretty brave—or foolhardy." An impish smile tilted her lips. "How do you know he wouldn't have cared?"

"Buddy said it was the best day of his life. On the back of that horse, high off the ground, he said he felt like he was flying. He said the freedom and exhilaration he'd experienced was worth a dozen lumps on the head. We sneaked him out to the stables a couple more times before we graduated. He loved it more each time he did it. Because we were going to different colleges, Buddy and I drifted apart. I hadn't seen or heard from him until he called me last year."

Marlo looked at him expectantly, waiting for him to go on.

"He'd found a center not far from his home that does equine-assisted stuff. He'd tried it again—with professionals this time—and loved it as much as ever. Buddy called me immediately and told me that if he'd had these experiences as a young child he believed it would have changed his life. The younger the child, the better the chance of significant improvement, he says.

"He insisted that I shouldn't waste the space and horses on the ranch but rather set up a program for children like he was. Kids who need to build strength, balance, increased range of motion and a burst of self-esteem."

She chewed on that for a moment, he noticed, before speaking again. "Not everyone rides a horse," she mused. "I can just imagine what a giddy high that would be for a child who'd been limited to a wheelchair."

He liked the way she thought. The program wasn't just about physical benefits, but about emotional ones, as well. Not everyone understood that. "Buddy is now on the board of that hippotherapy facility in New York. He's been helping—and hounding—me to get this done. I'm too committed to quit now. In the end, Dad will respect my decision, but not before he thinks of every possible thing that can go wrong with the plan."

"It must be fun to be him," Marlo murmured, under her breath.

Jake heard her and smiled. "I wouldn't walk a mile in his boots, if that's what you mean. Dad had a serious financial setback when I was just a kid. He almost lost the stables and hasn't been the same man since. My mother said he almost had a breakdown but he came back like gangbusters. He calls me too laid-back and easygoing. I call it rolling with the punches."

They drove in silence while Jake maneuvered through the heavy traffic. He could feel Marlo's eyes on him, covertly studying his profile, but he said nothing. She was scoping him out and he didn't blame her. He liked a cautious woman.

Jake felt every fiber in his body begin to relax as they turned off the interstate and wound their way through the western suburbs. This was the place he loved, where the land was dotted with barns and decorated with white chains of fence looping like necklaces across the rolling countryside.

He took a turn into a long, tree-canopied drive with white fencing undulating along both sides of the road and a tunnel of maple and linden branches, which shaded the drive that led to his childhood home. In front of her she could see a large red barn set like a ruby centerpiece in the emerald grass. As they neared, a gangly colt and its mother, inside an enclosure by the barn, came into view.

"It looks like June!" Marlo blurted. She sat bolt upright and stared straight ahead.

Jake glanced at her, confused. "What are you talking about?"

"Lucy gave me a calendar for Christmas. It is full of beautiful, placid scenes of animal mothers and their babies, a deer and fawn poking their noses out of a stand of trees, a dog nursing her puppies and a beautiful mare and foal…."

"And a mare and foal is the calendar photo for the month of June?"

"Exactly."

His lips tipped upward at the corners. "Following your train of thought is definitely a challenge."

"I suppose it's because my train keeps jumping the track."

He laughed out loud. "I enjoy you, Marlo. I've never met someone whose mind works quite like yours."

She sighed and sank back into her seat. "People tell me that all the time. My father says that God installed my logic backward. I say God doesn't make mistakes, so I must be okay."

"Very okay," he murmured, beneath his breath.

Jake slowed as he pulled up to the barn. Two men were standing in the open door, talking. "My father is still here, I see. He's going golfing with his friend Alfred, but obviously they haven't left yet. You met Alfred at the party. Dad and Alfred have been golfing together for forty years. We'll see how your logic works with my father. He thinks *my* sense is flawed. I'm interested to see what he thinks about *yours*."

"Jake, where is your mother?"

"Mom? She and her sister are in Europe. They go every year. My family is in constant motion. Then she and Dad will spend time together in Mexico. I'm the only one who likes it well enough to stay here through the winter." He regretted that sometimes. He was a family man at heart. He'd decided that long ago, but he lived in a world that didn't allow him time to cultivate that part of himself.

Jake watched Marlo step out of the car and onto grass mowed so perfectly that it reminded him of a well-groomed golf course. The pastures looked good, he noticed with approval, and the fences had been newly painted in a white so bright it could almost hurt a person's eyes.

Jake took her arm and steered her toward an outbuilding between two red, steel-fenced, round pens. "Currently, this shed is being used to store supplies, but we have plenty of room elsewhere to do that. This building will be the lounge and office for the hippotherapy program, a comfortable place for children and their families to wait their turns at the horses. It's near the round pens, so that if the rider's siblings want to watch television or play games, they will still be close to their parents. I plan to keep it simple. It's about the kids and the horses, nothing else. Well, what do you think?"

Keep it simple? Marlo took in the barns and storage buildings, the casually elegant landscaping, the row of black Range Rovers with Hammond Stables emblazoned on the sides in gold paint, the working Bobcats for cleaning barns, and fleet of black-and-gold horse trailers. If this was simple, she'd be curious to see what complex looked like.

Off to one side of the yard stood the family home, a stone and wood structure that spread out gracefully across a rise in the land, as if to survey the kingdom that was Hammond Stables. Mullioned windows, elaborately carved doors, chimneys hinting at multiple fireplaces and two large Irish setters lounging on the stone front steps made it look like a painting rather than an actual home.

"My father's house," Jake commented. "My grandparents also live there in a separate wing, but they are gone most of the year. The Hammond dynasty's headquarters." He said it so mockingly that Marlo turned to stare at him.

Seeing her wide eyes, he smiled a little. "Don't pay attention to me. I don't enjoy butting heads with the family to start the riding program. It seems to me that, with as much as our family has gained, they'd be a little more willing to give back."

Marlo didn't speak. The Hammond family dynamic was powerful, and she didn't understand the undercurrents. Neither did she want to be dragged out to sea without knowing what hit her. While she already felt as if she'd known Jake for years, he was almost a stranger to her—a charming, handsome, generous stranger, but a stranger nonetheless.

The two men who'd been talking by the barn moved toward them. There was no mistaking Jake's father—the lean, athletic build, broad shoulders, striking, pale-blue eyes, skin tanned and weathered from years in the sun and sharp, angular features. Randall Hammond wasn't the warm, fuzzy type. Maybe all those genes had been passed on to Jake through his mother.

He stared appraisingly at Marlo as he neared. To be given the once-over by Randall Hammond made her shiver, even on a warm day like this one. Then Randall smiled and the notion was shattered. Maybe Jake's innate charm *was* an inherited factor, she thought.

"Who have we here?" Randall asked pleasantly.

"You remember Marlo Mayfield, Dad. She's the owner of Dining with Divas, the catering group that did our last party."

"Oh, yes." Obviously, Randall had filed their meeting under "Insignificant and Unimportant," because he'd promptly forgotten who she was. "Be sure to leave more business cards on the counter in the office. Clients have been asking about the food."

"She's not here on business," Jake said, sounding annoyed. "I invited her out to show her the stables." He touched her shoulder protectively.

The other man, who'd been silent, chuckled. "You should know your father well enough by now, Jake. He's *always* doing business, even in his sleep."

"Marlo, this is my grandfather, Samuel. He and my grandmother are off tomorrow to the West Coast, where they have a second home."

The old man grabbed her hands in his and gave them a welcoming squeeze. She liked Samuel Hammond immediately. Here was Jake's real genetic benefactor. Even at his age, which had to be at least eighty, he stood tall and erect, almost with military bearing. Not a silver hair out of place, not a speck of dust on his pressed denims or cowboy boots, he looked like the peer of the realm, this vast stately horse operation.

"Are you interested in horses?" he asked genially.

"As a child I adored them, but anything I know I learned from reading a book. That isn't saying much, considering I was mildly dyslexic and reading wasn't easy for me. I'm thrilled to be here, though."

Samuel looked pleased to hear of her interest, but Randall frowned as if admitting to being dyslexic were a significant flaw, like bragging about a knock-kneed colt.

Smoothly Jake changed the subject. "I thought you were going to play golf today."

"I am." Randall sounded thoroughly disgusted. "If Alfred ever shows up. Apparently, his daughters, Jackie and Sabrina, thought they should have pedicures or some such nonsense. He agreed to watch his granddaughter Cammi until eleven. Every woman in that family has him wrapped around their finger, even the eight-year-old. You should talk to Sabrina about this, Jake. Alfred's run over by the women around him."

Jake smiled, but it was apparent that he had no interest in taking on all the Dorchester women at once, either. Smart man.

Since blonde, possessive Sabrina was the daughter of Randall Hammond's best friend, it was no wonder that she had an exclusive on Jake. Given her slightly younger age, she'd probably grown up idolizing the older, handsome boy that Jake no doubt had been. Sabrina had likely staked her claim on him years ago.

To Marlo's amazement, she felt disappointed by the knowledge. What gave her the right to be unhappy to know this man was already taken? Jealousy was hardly her style. It wasn't as if they actually *knew* each other. After Angela's announcement, she'd had become painfully aware of her marital status—or lack thereof.

Get a grip! Marlo squared her shoulders. She'd come here to see horses and learn about a program to help children, not to lasso a man.

Thankfully, at that moment a groom led a young horse out of the barn and toward a nearby round pen. The animal's flanks rippled with muscle and glinted like bronze in the sunlight, and the creature turned to look at the small group with soft, liquid-brown eyes that took Marlo's breath away.

"He's beautiful. I think I'm in love!"

"That's Shaker, as in Keeps Them Shaking in Their Boots. Good breeding, nice form. He's quite a boy." Randall was suddenly the profoundly proud papa of this handsome four-legged prize. "I have great hopes for this one. His bloodlines are impeccable."

"Don't get your hopes up too much, Dad. You once had high hopes for me, too." Jake beckoned the groom over, and when they neared, he offered his hand, palm down, to the horse to sniff.

His grandfather Samuel chuckled, but Randall gave a snort that startled the horse.

"It's only lately that I've been questioning you," Randall said bluntly. "Since you got this cockamamie notion to haul little kids here and let them ride our horses. What if one of the horses were to get hurt…or even one of the kids? Our animals aren't big dogs for kids to play on."

Marlo caught the clear indication that Randall's concern was for the horses first and the children second. It wasn't lost on Jake either.

"We'll only use older riding horses, not show animals. Just a couple of the bomb-proof ones to start."

"'Bomb-proof?'" Marlo queried. "What is that?"

"Experienced horses that have had a lot of riding time, like retired police or show horses. 'Bomb-proof' means they can tolerate firecrackers and police sirens in a parade, walk over a sheet of tin or see a small animal jump out of the grass in front of them and not shy. I consider them reliable and dependable. Nothing flighty or restless."

"There are horses like that?"

"The fact remains that they are still animals, so there are no hundred-percent guarantees, but in the atmosphere of an enclosed riding arena, the likelihood of one of them spooking is little to none."

"Maybe even *I* could ride a horse like that. For my first time on a horse, I'll probably need a bomb-proof—or perhaps comatose—animal."

"Of course you can ride. Most of the riders will be very young and have disabilities. You'll be fine. If not, I'll help you."

Marlo would have pondered that pleasant idea for a moment longer, but Randall made a sound in his throat like that of an angry bull. "Do you have an idea what kind of liability insurance we'll have to carry for a half-baked idea like this?"

"It's already in the works." Jake's voice was utterly calm.

Randall's complexion grew ruddy beneath his tan, and Marlo saw how upset he was.

"What happens on the back of a horse that can't happen in a physical therapy program?" Obviously, Randall didn't entertain the notion that this might be a success. "You got this do-goody stuff from your mother," Randall said, in a tone that bordered on disgust. He turned on his heel and stalked off toward the sprawling house. Samuel said nothing, but followed him, shaking his head.

When he was gone, Jake turned to Marlo and grinned. "Now you see where I got all my innate charm."

"I do see where you got your good looks. I suspect your charm is a direct inheritance from your grandfather." Even as she said it, Marlo realized that she'd been far too blunt. "I didn't mean that your father doesn't have charm, exactly…he just didn't have it on display today…I mean…. I've put my foot in it now, haven't I?"

"And a rather pretty foot it is. Don't feel badly. Deep down inside, my father has a genuine streak of compassion and generosity. I'm counting on it. This project is too important to stop now. Like I said, the Hammonds are blessed with wealth and good fortune. It's time to give some of it back. I'm meant to do this. I believe God's hand is on it. Once Dad sees how well the program does and the goodwill it generates, he'll begin to realize that instead of hurting Hammond Farms, it will give it a new dimension. Perhaps it will be one that may even enhance our reputation."

"So if it buys goodwill and good advertising, he'll like it?"

"It's not exactly the way I'd like him to embrace it, but if that's what it takes, okay. He'll come around eventually. My dad would lay down his life for friends and family," Jake said softly, as if compelled to explain his father to her. "Especially for Alfred. They've always had each other's backs. They'd do anything for each other. It was Alfred who helped him back to solvency many years ago. Dad would—and did—promise him anything, including his first born, if necessary."

"How about you? It doesn't appear he'll do just 'anything' for you."

Jake grinned. "Oh, my dad would die for me, if necessary. It's just that he's not all that willing to *agree* with me."

Chapter Eight

Chandeliers in a barn?

Marlo trailed Jake inside a vast cavern that smelled like fresh hay and leather polish. Above her was a series of crystal chandeliers. Soft music played in each of the roomy wood and metal temperature-controlled horse stalls. The floors were covered with interlocking stall mats. Air-conditioning…elegant accoutrements…Mozart and Bach…these horses lived a lifestyle more stylish than she did!

"What's wrong with this picture?" she blurted.

The corners of Jake's eyes crinkled in amusement. He, of lean frame and tanned good looks, appeared right at home in this unexpected opulence. "The animals like the temperature and the padding under their feet, but the chandeliers are for the clients. We could have the same fine horses in a ramshackle barn, but potential buyers would turn up their noses. Think of it as marketing."

"Horse snobbery?"

"Just don't say that in front of my father. He's a master snob when it comes to Hammond Stables. He has an eye for horseflesh like no other, but he gave up mucking stalls and building fence a long time ago. That's left to the hired hands."

"They are your cleaning service for barns, then."

"You could say that. And my father is as fastidious about how the barns are kept as my mother is about her house."

"You don't seem particularly excited about your own business."

"I share a passion for horses with my father and grandfather—especially now that I've decided to build the therapy center. I, however, am just as happy on the back of a horse purchased at an auction without a pedigree as on a stallion with a lineage to rival that of Queen Elizabeth.

"I've had two calls this morning, both from therapists with hippotherapy experience. They have agreed to work with us as much and as often as they can. By next Saturday we should have a few kids here to ride." Marlo could almost feel the excitement vibrating within him as he spoke. She was drawn to his passion like a moth to a flame.

Then a shadow crossed his features. "Between now and then I have to convince my father that my plan isn't going to send Hammond Stables spiraling out of its hard-won stature."

Marlo was about to respond when she felt a firm, warm pressure between her shoulder blades, which sent her stumbling toward the middle of the barn aisle. "Hey!" She regained her balance and turned toward her assailant. An inky black mare with soft brown eyes peered at her curiously, her finely shaped head framed above the half door to her stall.

"Don't mind Twisty, she greets everyone who gets close to her stall that way." Jake walked over to scratch the beautifully shaped nose. Twisty pushed it deep into his palm. "Don't you, sweetheart?" he purred. He stroked the finely curved neck and scratched beneath her forelock as if he knew exactly where the animal liked to be touched. "What a beautiful girl you are." His voice was little more than a purr as he whispered to the mare.

Marlo soon realized she was envious of a horse.

The sound of an approaching car and a commotion outside short-circuited their tour. A familiar little girl suddenly bolted into the stable. She was dressed in a riding habit, jodpur breeches, high black boots, white shirt and a black velveteen helmet. Long blond curls tumbled randomly down her back. "I came for my riding lesson," she announced imperiously, and tossed her head. "Grandpa brought me."

"Hello, Cammi." Jake sounded amused by the haughty little princess. "Do you remember my friend Marlo?"

"Yes." Cammi stalked over on her tiny, booted feet to shake Marlo's hand. "Not a *girlfriend*, I hope. Auntie Sabrina wouldn't like that."

Jake swallowed a chuckle. "A *friend* friend, Cammi, not that it's any of your business. Mind your manners."

"Is my granddaughter bothering you?" A tall, slender man walked through the barn door. Framed in the sunlight behind him, Marlo was unable to see his face, but she still recognized Randall's friend Alfred.

"Alfred, this is Marlo Mayfield."

"Yes, we met at your party. Nice to see you again, Marlo." He gave a courtly hint of a bow before turning to Jake. Alfred turned to the little blonde princess beside him. "And of course you know Cammi, who is not the least bit shy."

Cammi gave the sparest hint of a curtsy before grabbing her grandfather's hand. "I want to ride now, Grampy. Now."

He sighed. "Honey, your mother and Sabrina should be here shortly. Then you can ride. Randall and I are going golfing."

A petite storm cloud appeared to form on Cammi's face, but Jake, obviously aware of the pitfalls of allowing this to happen, interjected, "Cammi, we just put a new flat-screen television in the office between the round pens. Seems to me there are a couple video games hooked up if you want…"

The little girl was gone in a flurry of flying blond curls.

Clever. Check.

Marlo sighed as Cammi disappeared out the door. Sabrina was about to arrive at any moment: The day had taken a decidedly discouraging turn.

"Maybe we'd better get going," Marlo hinted. "Looks like everyone has places to go."

"I'm not done showing you the stables." Jake's words were barely audible over the sound of a car coming to a screeching halt in front of the barn doors.

Too late, Marlo thought. Competition for Jake's attention arrived before she had time to escape.

Sabrina posed dramatically in the doorway of the barn for her grand entrance. Her eyes found Jake's immediately, and she glided toward him, smiling coyly. She was dressed in jeans more costly than Marlo's entire outfit, and a pale orange sweater that draped casually off one shoulder. The color was highly flattering to her peaches-and-cream complexion.

Sabrina caught a glimpse of Marlo and her step faltered. Then she recovered her poise and attached herself to Jake like a bug to flypaper and kissed him on the cheek.

Why does Jake buy into this nonsense? Marlo wondered. Maybe it had something to do with the fact that she was as accustomed to wealth and privilege as Jake was. Suddenly, Marlo felt as out of place with Jake as one of her aunt Tildy's lawn ornaments in the Queen's gardens.

Jake noticed the quicksilver change of expression on Marlo's face. She didn't look entirely pleased. Sabrina's spectacular beauty had that effect on women sometimes. Sabrina had nothing over Marlo in the beauty department, he thought, the lovely caterer probably just didn't realize it.

"So you are still going ahead with that project of yours?" Alfred asked.

"My father hasn't talked me out of it, if that's what you mean," Jake said genially. "You can admit that he's told you that's what he wants to do."

"Maybe you can talk some sense into him, Alfred," Randall said. "Disabled kids learning to ride while show horses are being trained? In my mind, they just don't mix." He turned to his son. "Jake, you don't even know what you're getting into!"

"And you do, Dad? At least give me a chance. It's going to work out."

"If you like kids so much, why don't you settle down, marry Sabrina and have some of your own? I don't know why you've waited this long. I suppose you're too much like your grandmother. All heart, no common sense."

This was an old conversation between them. Randall had expected Sabrina to be his future daughter-in-law from the day she was born.

"Let's not be unpleasant." Startling him, Sabrina hooked her arm around Jake's. "Jake is a smart businessman. If he thinks this will work, then it will."

"I'm not starting a *business* exactly. Just…"

"Charity, then." She waved a manicured hand. "Whatever. If my Jake is in charge, it will work out."

He noticed Marlo cringe at the word *charity*. He would have to have a private conversation with Sabrina about her choice of words and the careless way she and the others were discussing his plan. Sadly, none of them except Marlo seemed to have any idea what he was trying to do. There were too many children who could be helped by hippotherapy for him to sit silently on the sidelines doing nothing. What was more, he'd prayed for direction, and this was what God had given him. It had been put in his heart, and he was not about it ignore it.

Sabrina moved closer to Jake and tilted her head upward to gaze soulfully into his eyes. "I'm so proud of you, honey," she said, effectively marking her territory with a huge *Keep Off, He's Mine* sign directed unswervingly at Marlo.

Still thinking of the challenge his father might present to the success of the program, Jake didn't notice.

Chapter Nine

"So, you are going to see if Brady can ride, even though his mother wants nothing to do with it?" Lucy asked, as she and Marlo worked side by side in the Divas kitchen.

"She wants nothing to do with it so far, but I'm not done asking yet." She had suggested that Brady might try Jake's program. "Maybe he'd receive some real benefit from riding, Jenny," she'd told her sister. "Imagine Brady on the back of a horse! He loves animals. You know he's crazy about your neighbor's dog."

"That's a dog, Marlo, not a horse," Jenny had responded tersely.

"It's the size of a horse. What is it, half Great Dane and half St. Bernard?"

"Don't be flip. He'd be terrified. You know how fragile he is, Marlo."

It wasn't Brady who would be terrified, but his mother, Marlo thought. Jenny guarded her son like he was a Fabergé egg. She wasn't convinced that her sister was doing her son any favors by keeping him wrapped in cotton batting. He was a little boy who deserved to live as normal a life as possible. Then again, she'd never walked in Jenny's shoes.

"So Jenny wouldn't go for it?"

"She almost hung up on me."

"Then that's that. Now tell me what else is wrong. I can see it in your eyes."

"Tired, that's all. I couldn't sleep last night." Marlo piped frosting onto cupcakes to make them look like clown faces for a child's upcoming birthday party.

"It's been over two weeks since you've heard from him, right?" Lucy sipped her tea. Then she looked at Marlo with compassion. "You really like him, don't you?"

"I hardly know him, but, yes, I do like him—a lot. And unfortunately, he's so totally taken."

"Does he act as crazy about Sabrina as she is about him?"

"It seems pretty one-sided, but everyone speaks openly about the two of them being together." She recalled Randall's admonition to Jake to hurry up and marry Sabrina. "Their families are so tightly connected that it feels inevitable. Randall and Alfred have clearly been planning this union since Sabrina was in the cradle."

"He's a big boy. He can decide for himself who he wants to marry. He may be interested in you, too. After all, he asked you to volunteer in the program."

"I will probably never know. I refuse to throw myself at him. It's inappropriate." She hadn't dreamed she'd meet someone with the qualifications of Prince Charming. Ironically, she had, but he was taken. *Now what?* she wondered.

"You are seeing Bryan soon, aren't you?" Lucy asked.

Marlo gave her a dirty look and Lucy made a gesture of zipping her mouth shut. Marlo and Bryan were the perfect uncouple. He was a blond and she was dark, he was as tanned as she was pale. They shared athleticism, the same alma mater and a slightly skewed sense of humor. Bryan had been one of Marlo's best friends ever since he'd rescued her shovel and bucket from a bully in the sandbox. The idea of being romantically inclined toward Bryan—or Bryan toward her—was ludicrous.

Besides, he was currently enamored with Marlo's cousin, Kelly, a pretty young thing who had enlisted in the army and was off at boot camp. Kelly had left behind instructions that Marlo was to watch over Bryan for her, knowing that Marlo's were the safest possible hands in which to leave him.

"He's hardly a date. I'm his suit of armor while Kelly is away. My job is to deflect women who find Bryan appealing, remember?"

"No one needs to know that. In fact, it might do Jake Hammond some good to see you with Bryan. Maybe he's the jealous type."

"You've got this entire thing out of proportion, Lucy. I've agreed to work with the program he's developing. That's it. Don't try to make something out of this that it isn't."

Lucy didn't even blink. "But you're falling for him, I can tell. I've seen you through every boyfriend you've ever had, but there's something different about this."

"There certainly is." Marlo was becoming annoyed with the conversation. "He's taken. If I learned just one thing in the debacle over Jeremiah, it's that women need to learn to keep their hands to themselves. Now, if you'll excuse me, I have work to do."

"Okay, be that way, but mark my words, the electricity between the two of you will only grow. I see sparks already." Before Marlo could protest, Lucy added, "I'm leaving for a dental appointment. While you're alone here, think about what I've said." She slipped quickly out the back door and was gone, leaving Marlo to consider the very thing she wanted to ignore.

The bell rang, signaling that someone had entered Dining with Divas. Marlo, wiping her hands on her apron, poked her head around the corner. "May I help you... Jake!"

He shoved his hands deep into his pockets, suddenly feeling

schoolboyishly shy. "I thought you might wonder if I'd dropped off the face of the planet by now." Even with flour on her nose and her hair appearing to have been combed in a wind tunnel she was incredibly appealing. He wanted very much to think she hadn't forgotten him.

"It has been a few days."

Sixteen, actually…and fourteen hours, Jake thought.

She ambled into the front office, unaware that she had flour dusting her clothes as well as her face. Jake found it utterly charming, as he did with most things about her. "I've been waiting for a call to come to Hammond Stables and work with the horses and children."

He hoped it had felt as long to her as it had to him…an eternity. "There's been a holdup. I hate to admit that my father was right, but the insurance has been a sticking point. I thought we had it covered, but everything was put on hold until we could work out a couple details."

"When do I start? Side-walking with the kids and horses, I mean."

"I'll have to let you know. By Monday at the latest." He felt foreign in his architect clothes today, very crisp and professional in a charcoal-gray suit and red-and-gray power tie. He wanted to be in denim.

"Oh." Her face fell and the animation in her eyes dimmed.

"You look disappointed."

"I am. Even though we are plenty busy with the business, I've thought about the horses a lot."

"That reminds me. My father has investors coming in next weekend that he wants to impress. He asked me to arrange for you to cater the meal. Can you do it?" Jake pulled a slip of paper from an inner pocket in his jacket. "Here are the details. Note that these men are bringing their families—much to my father's dismay."

Marlo looked puzzled. "I'm not sure I understand."

"Dad is of the old school—children should be seen and not heard—or, better yet, left at home with a sitter. I hope you can accommodate the kids, too." He moved close enough to notice that she smelled wonderful, like almonds and vanilla. It took everything in his power to keep from wrapping her in his arms and inhaling the sweetness.

She took a step backward and he mentally berated himself for moving too quickly. He should have known better. She was skittish, like a colt.

"And after this is over I'd like to spend a little time with you and the horses, so you feel comfortable when the children come for therapy." He liked the way her blue eyes lit at the suggestion.

"Let's check the calendar. It's in my office."

Jake trailed her into the small room which housed the Divas' cookbook library. "If you made every recipe in every one of these books, how long would it take?" Jake asked, examining the floor-to-ceiling bookshelves.

"A couple of lifetimes, probably."

"Then why have so many?"

"I'm addicted. I write fan letters to cookbook authors." She looked up from the calendar and grinned. "You're the first person to whom I've ever admitted that."

"I can understand why," he said, teasing, but liked the idea.

"Don't you collect anything?"

Jake thought for a moment. It had been a long time since he'd had Matchbox cars or autographed baseballs. "Horses, I guess."

"And you think *my* collection is odd? I can buy a cookbook more cheaply than you can feed and house just one of your collection for a day."

"I also have photos of the greats—Triple Crown winners like Assault, Affirmed and Kincsem, the European racehorse that won all fifty-four of her races. Does that count? But your point is well taken. We're both quirky in one way or another."

He had the good sense not to add "but you're far more quirky than I am." It was probably true, since he was often accused of being a "straight arrow," but he was glad he hadn't said it. For some odd reason, he felt the urge to protect this intelligent, capable woman—from *what,* he had no idea. She was just the kind he might lay his coat over a mud puddle for, or gallop in to rescue on a big white horse. He couldn't explain it, but it was the sense he had. She made him feel like a knight in shining armor. Odd. Very odd.

"Okay," she said, as she scrawled on her calendar. "That day is all yours. How many are coming? Should we do a sit-down dinner?"

"No, they'll be there for lunch. There are four in the group. If they bring their wives, that makes eight. I'm nine and my father makes ten. My grandfather and grandmother are leaving for a three-month-long cruise, so they won't attend."

"I'll plan for extra. That way you can invite others at the last minute. If no one else comes, you can have seconds. Now, about those children…"

Jake's cell phone rang. "Jake here." He listened to one of his foremen and frowned. "Okay, I'll be right over." He folded the little phone and put it into his pocket. "Trouble on a building site. I've got to go. We'll talk later. Maybe over dinner. I'll trust you to figure out something for the kids." He grabbed her hand, squeezing it as he smiled at her, then tore himself away and strode for the door. He could feel her eyes on his back, watching him go.

Marlo told herself to get over it as she got into her car and headed for her sister's house. Jake wasn't the man for her. That was wishful thinking, a true fairy tale. Besides, the Divas' general rule was not to mix business with pleasure. She didn't dare let too much pleasure intrude. Both the Divas' financial bottom line and her integrity demanded it.

Jenny and Brady were in the front yard when Marlo pulled into their driveway.

"Auntie Marlo!" Brady's face beamed like sunshine breaking through the clouds.

She scooped the child into her arms and he clung enthusiastically to her neck. Gently, she pried one arm away so she could breathe. "How's my favorite boy?" she asked.

"Good." He put a small hand on each of her cheeks, squished them together and giggled. "You look funny."

"Thanks a bunch." Marlo put Brady down on the grass and he meandered off to pick up the large blue ball he and his mother had been rolling across the lawn.

"We're working on Brady's coordination," Jenny said. "It's coming along."

"What would you think if I told you there might be another way to help with that?"

"Are you bringing up that horse thing again? Give it up, Marlo. I won't put my child on the top of some huge beast!"

"Horses are hardly *beasts,* Jenny."

"If Brady were yours, you'd have a different opinion." Jenny's soft features hardened, the mother lion in her surfacing.

"In a way, he *is* mine, sis. You know how much I love him."

Some of Jenny's ire dissipated. "I know. You've been his protector as long as I have, but I'm so terrified that he'll be hurt."

"What if you hurt him by sheltering him so much? You'll make him as afraid for himself as you are for him. You've got to give him an opportunity to grow."

Jenny laid a hand on Marlo's arm. "If I change my mind you'll be the first to know. Until then…"

Her sister would never agree, Marlo thought. Not in a million years.

Marlo's cell phone rang. "Excuse me, Jen, I'd better take this.

"Dining with Divas. Hungry? Let's dish!" Lucy insisted that they say something clever each time they answered the phone. Marlo felt as witty as a stump, but the clients seemed to think it was endearing.

"It's Jake Hammond."

She winced. "Ignore what I just said."

His chuckle rolled across the airwaves. "Why? It's kind of cute."

Coming from him, she almost believed it.

"Dad wanted me to be sure that you'd thought of something to 'do' with the children on Saturday. He doesn't see how he can conduct business with kids running around." Jake chuckled humorlessly. "If he doesn't want *clients* to bring kids to the stables, you can see how enthusiastic he must be about my 'lunatic idea.'"

"Tell him I'll make it work," Marlo murmured, her mind whirring. "If I can't think of a solution, then I don't deserve to be a Diva."

Chapter Ten

Marlo catapulted out of her car and hurried toward Jake, looking so intent and businesslike that he had to suppress a smile. She always made him feel like smiling. Her animated features, expressive blue eyes and unique take on the world gave Jake more pleasure than he'd had in a long time. Her unapologetic candor and genuine unaffectedness delighted him. He'd be willing, Jake realized, to do even more of the entertaining he usually disliked, just to keep her around.

The first thing out of her mouth was "How about a scavenger hunt? Lucy and I will run the hunt while you and your father conduct business."

"Good morning to you, too." He watched an attractive pink color wash over her cheeks. "You can do all this?"

"We charge extra for babysitting," Marlo said cheerfully.

"If you can keep the kids, their parents *and* my father happy, I'll pay you double."

"I like people willing to try new things. It's a deal." She made a check mark in the air with her finger.

It probably meant something, Jake thought, but he had no idea what.

"I'm not very well acquainted with horsey things," she continued. "If you really want the children to feel like they know Hammond Farms, I'll need your help."

"I believe we'll need coffee to get this done." Jake tipped his head toward the house. "Let's go inside and work on it." He took her arm and guided her along the stone paving that led to the home. Someday he hoped to live here, when his father and mother decided that it was their turn to retire. Unfortunately, most of the women he knew wouldn't love it like he did. Too far out in the country for most, too far from urban life, this place demanded a special person to enjoy a community where the majority of the population had four feet rather than two.

He opened the large carved door that led to the dusky interior. "Perhaps you'd like to step out on the deck while I get some coffee."

He left her looking at the view and returned with a tray containing a carafe of coffee, two mugs and a plate of sugar cookies. When she heard him at the door she spun around. Her eyes were wide and dancing with delight. "What an incredible view!"

"I know what you mean. It's my favorite spot in the house. We'll use the sunroom. It's perfect in there this time of day." He led her to the large four-season porch filled with wicker furniture, plush pillows and a greenhouse worth of flowers. Pastures flanked them on three sides.

"Why do you ever leave this place? It's incredible."

"It would be crowded, for one thing. As I said, my grandparents live in one wing, my parents in the other. I can't quite imagine myself caught in the middle of this house, with my father and grandfather offering stereo suggestions as to what I should do with my life. In their eyes, I've never quite grown up— and never will." The thought made him cringe. "That alone was enough to make me buy my own home."

He put down the tray and began to pour coffee. "I've learned to roll with the punches and not let anything bother me too much. The older my father gets, however, the more uptight he becomes. He sees problems behind every tree and bush these days, and wants to control everything around him."

"I understand. My family is bossy enough, and I'm not even in business with them." She rolled her eyes and smiled.

"Tell me about your family." Jake found himself genuinely interested.

"My parents live in Wisconsin, where they run a fishing resort. It's their dream—Dad gets to fish and Mom gets to cook for fishermen. I learned how to cook from my mother and enjoy it *almost* as much as she does. I have an older brother in California who has no children, and a sister here in the Minneapolis area. She's the mother of my nephew, Brady."

"Are you close?"

"We're crazy about each other, if that's what you mean. Of course, they'd all tell you that they are very normal compared to me. They never read the last page of the book first."

"You do that?" Amusement deepened the smile lines around his eyes. Even the way she bounced all over the map when speaking charmed him.

"They can all read maps and drive better forward than they do in reverse."

Jake's curiosity was piqued, and he wanted to ask more questions. Discovering all there was about Marlo could occupy him for weeks, he was sure. Maybe years. Unfortunately, the issue at hand was still Saturday's luncheon.

"Where do we start with these clues? I have to confess that I've never been on a scavenger hunt."

"Then you suffered a deprived childhood," Marlo said firmly. "This will be good for you. Just name some spots around the property that could be on the hunt. The kids will get a clue to start the game. When they solve the riddle and go to the spot hinted at in the clue, they'll find another clue." Marlo pulled a pencil and a notebook out of her pocket and looked at him expectantly.

Did she know she narrowed her eyes when she asked questions? Or that one corner of her mouth had a comic tilt? Probably not.

He furrowed his brow as he rattled off a string of suggestions. "Riding arena, round pen, paddocks, tack room, water tank, hay loft…"

"What are the half-doors in the barn called? The split doors I saw closed at the bottom and open at the top."

"Dutch, or stable doors. They were originally meant to keep animals out of homes while letting light and air in. Now they're used in barns."

"That's a great place to start."

She wrote a few words, frowned, crossed them out, tapped the eraser end of the pencil on the table and repeated the process until, finally, she held up the battered piece of paper triumphantly. "Here." She handed it to him to read it out loud.

"'We're not in the Netherlands, but you can find these all over the barn. Look to the west, where outside meets in.'" He handed the sheet back to her. "I don't get it."

"That's because you haven't thought about it. What are the people of the Netherlands called?"

"The Dutch, of course."

"And where might the outside of something—like a building—meet the inside?"

Puzzled, Jake felt like a child trying to figure this out, in order to win a game or capture a prize. "Walls, windows, doors…"

"Exactly!" She clapped delightedly.

"I don't quite see…."

"Dutch doors!" she crowed, as if the fog had been swept away by the sun. "The next clue for the hunt can be found by the Dutch door on the west side of the barn!"

He grabbed the paper and reread the clue.

"'We're not in the Netherlands but you can find these all over the barn. Look to the west, where outside meets in.'

"Isn't that a little difficult for kids to figure out?"

"Lucy and I will be there to help. You'd be surprised what children know."

"When you were a child, did you know what a Dutch door was?"

"Maybe not, but I knew about the Netherlands, and I knew east from west—sort of. The first thing I'd do with a clue like that is check out the west side of your barn. They won't even have to know what the rest means, because, if they're smart, they'll *see* the spot to pick up their next clue."

"Very clever. You just thought of all that?" The energy that bubbled out of Marlo was catching.

"It isn't hard. In my mind, I imagined a clue being just outside one of the barn doors. That made me think of how they are split, so the bottom can be closed without closing the top. Dutch doors. Then it was an easy leap to the Netherlands. I know it sounds backward, but it works for me."

"Just let me watch you work. Don't tell me anything about how you get to the clues. You make very expressive faces while you're thinking."

"Lucy says that, because my logic runs backward rather than forward, I have to strain to come up with something."

"I'm not touching that statement with a ten-foot pole."

While Jake refilled the coffee carafe, Marlo picked another of the items on his list. When he returned to the room she handed him her notebook. He stared at the clue written in the middle of the page.

It rhymes with a smelly fish but you'll find horses there.

"A smelly fish? That's no help. And there are horses every-where around here. In the stalls, being worked in round pens, in the paddock…." He paused and a big grin spread across his features. "A smelly fish is a haddock, so you'd find the next clue in a paddock!"

"Now you're catching on." Marlo beamed at him as if he were an elementary student who'd just seen the light in understanding fractions. "And, no, it isn't too hard. The kids can work backward. Besides, the harder clues will take more time to solve. They can find all the places there are horses and then ask the stable guys what they're called. Paddock-haddock will be easy then."

Jake leaned forward and laid his hand over Marlo's small hand. It was warm, delicate and oh-so-appealing. "You amaze me at every turn. What more is there to discover about you?" A powerful attraction tugged at him and he removed his hand quickly.

What was it about her that made him feel like the tide, help-lessly ebbing and flowing as she, the moon and sun, lured him? That was the last thing he'd expected to be served up by his caterer.

Marlo held on to the steering wheel, eyes straight ahead, radio blaring and her mind even noisier. Spending yesterday after-noon with Jake had done something to her head. Her brain was doing cartwheels as she tried to sort out her feelings. Did Jake think their relationship might continue even if Dining with Divas left the picture, or was he just planning social events for clients long into the future? He'd certainly been friendly, but maybe she was reading something into his smiles that wasn't really there. What about Sabrina? Marlo wasn't sure, but it made her uncom-fortable. Maybe he was just very good at flirting. He'd obviously had lots of practice.

He'd touched her hand for a brief moment and it had set a

crazy avalanche of emotions into action. Mental pictures raced through her head—she and Jake at the barns, brushing colts, laughing over dinner, holding hands, lips touching…. She shook herself like a wet dog, as if to fling the images as far away from her as possible. It was outlandish and unwise to think like that.

Much as she hated to admit it, Sabrina and Jake together made sense. Their families had been friends forever. They were part of the horsey set. Wealth was familiar to them. Their expectations were far different from her own.

Marlo's idea of success was to own a business in which she did not have to cook, tote, carry, serve and clean up every day. Having an employee sounded like a radical luxury to her. That was a far cry from running an architectural firm and owning a horse ranch that sat on land worth millions.

Forbidden fruit, that was what Jake was. Not only was he involved with someone else, but he was out of Marlo's league.

No, she'd better accept reality right now, she thought unhappily, and prevent the man from drawing her in. It would save her a lot of pain and frustration in the future. Jake and Sabrina were destined to be Mr. and Mrs. Hammond, and she wasn't about to interfere with that. Marlo was nothing if not practical.

"We have a Thanksgiving wedding to cater," Lucy said, when Marlo walked into the Divas' kitchen on Monday morning. "It's going to be a big one. Mammoth, gargantuan, colossal." She leaned back in her chair and tapped her front tooth with the tip of her pen. "And if I'm right, it is going to be one huge pain in the neck."

"Refuse it." Marlo picked up a fresh apron and put it on. "We do well enough. If something looks like trouble, we don't have to take it."

"Oh, there will be even more trouble if we don't accept, mark my words."

"Who are these people, Lucy? What's the problem?" She poured herself a mug of coffee and topped it with cream.

"It's Angela's wedding I'm talking about."

"Oh, no." Suddenly feeling leaden, Marlo sank onto a stool. "Angela is the most exacting, difficult-to-please human being on the planet. Her wedding will make a space launch look simple."

"Exactly. She's already been on the phone three times this morning, giving me instructions. Edible flowers on every plate. No shrimp in the reception hall because her family is allergic. And could we please consider buying new dishes if we don't have enough matching china? She wants the tables to be uniform. Oh, yes, she wants us to create centerpieces for the tables, as well. Edible ones. Bouquets of fresh fruit and cookies. And wait until you hear about the ice sculptures."

Marlo put her head in her hands. "What did we do to deserve this?"

"It's really nice of her to throw such a big event our way, even though it's going to be a logistical nightmare. But that's not the worst of it."

"There's more?" Marlo was already trying to imagine how they could keep edible centerpieces fresh. The apples and bananas would turn brown unless they bathed them in pineapple or lemon juice. If Angela wanted fruit and cookies mixed in each bouquet it was inevitable that the cookies would get soggy, unless she could figure out a way to apply a hard frosting…. "How could there be more?"

"She's asking every one of us from the Bridesmaid Club to be *her* bridesmaid, as well."

Soggy brown centerpieces flew out of Marlo's mind and were replaced by a new vision. Her, wrestling trays of chicken à la orange and tomato aspic in a shiny purple bridesmaid's dress with a peplum, two miles of ruffles and a matching hat. Hollywood made entire horror movies out of scenes less scary than that.

For the first time in a long time, Marlo felt vulnerable. Maybe this time, considering her emotions toward Jake, the upcoming scavenger hunt which could easily become a regrettable fiasco and Angela's unrelenting wedding demands, she'd taken on too much.

Chapter Eleven

"This crazy, harebrained scheme is not going to work." Randall's tanned face had darkened to a dangerous beet color. "We have four couples and nine children between the ages of seven and fifteen arriving in less than two hours. You expect me to be able to talk business and show horses while you and those kids are running wild around here on a scavenger hunt?"

He glared at Jake, who, coffee cup in hand, was visibly, at least, unperturbed about the paternal eruption. "Why didn't you tell me this before now?"

"Because I knew what your response would be," Jake said, thankful that he'd cultivated the ability to let all his father's comments roll off his back.

Randall spun on his heel to face Marlo, who was divesting the Dining with Divas van of cases of soda and paper products. "This is your fault. He wouldn't have had a crackpot idea like this on his own."

Much to Jake's delight, Marlo didn't shrink back as his father had obviously expected, but faced him, her feet firmly planted on the ground. "Excuse me for saying so, sir, but I wouldn't underestimate Jake," she said pleasantly. "From what I've observed, he has plenty of half-baked ideas of his own."

Randall blinked at the unexpected reply. Then he threw his hands in the air and stomped off, muttering, "Kids and business do not mix. I should just call this meeting off. I don't care how wealthy these investors are…."

Jake gave her a thumbs-up. "Good for you. You didn't let Dad run all over you."

She smiled at his encouragement. "Is he always this grouchy? Maybe he needs more fiber in his diet."

Jake nearly spit out his coffee. When he caught his breath, he put the mug down on top of a fence post. "Maybe he does, but I'm not going to be the one to tell him that. Dad was an only child. I'm his only child. He has no grandchildren. I really don't think he knows what to do with children. The only child I've ever seen him enjoy is Alfred's granddaughter, Cammi. He adores her. I think a group of children actually intimidates him."

"Fair enough," Marlo said. "But it's my job is to keep the children busy so he *can* show these investors they can have faith in his operation."

"Unfortunately you're outside Dad's concept of intelligent business practices. He doesn't know quite what to make of you." Just like Marlo was outside all his own experiences, too, Jake thought, but he was intrigued, not dismayed, by her uniqueness.

"Welcome to my world," Marlo said, with mock weariness. "For some reason, I affect people that way. I guess most business plans don't involve much *fun*."

He couldn't—didn't want to—resist. Jake wrapped his arm around her shoulder and gave her a squeeze. His cheek rested against her dark hair, which smelled of strawberries. "That's what I love about you, Marlo—the fun."

It was in his nature to be affectionate, but Marlo had the

ability to test his gentlemanly restraint, he realized, and pulled his arm away. He'd laughed when Sabrina had brought up the way he responded to Marlo, discounting what she'd called her "woman's intuition." Maybe there was something to those feminine hunches after all. It was disconcerting to consider.

"I'm done setting up the clues." Lucy chugged toward them like a little steam engine. "We're ready for your guests to arrive, Jake."

"If we can pull this off to my father's satisfaction, I'm taking you ladies out to dinner—you pick the restaurant and I'll spare no expense."

"Then I'd better recheck Marlo's plan. I don't want to miss an opportunity like that." Lucy turned and trotted off again.

"I'd better see to the main table," Marlo said quickly—as if she, too, sensed the electricity between them. "If these people are driving in from the airport, they'll probably be ready to eat immediately after they arrive."

So the encounter had disconcerted her, as well. It was obvious to Jake that whatever he might say about the two of them, she didn't want to hear it. She was probably right. They were on a friendly, even keel. No use rocking the boat.

Shortly, cars began to pull into the driveway, and out tumbled an array of adults and children who appeared to have been outfitted by Ralph Lauren.

Before Jake stepped forward to greet their guests, he eyed the group. It would be easy to make the adults feel at home. The youngsters, however, had *boring* written all over their faces. What if Marlo's plan didn't work? These were privileged children, accustomed to whatever money could buy. Maybe a scavenger hunt would be laughable to them. He winced at the thought.

Randall Hammond waved Marlo over to the group and Jake watched her cross the yard. She might have had lead in her shoes, for all he knew, the way she was dragging her feet. She must have had an attack of nerves, as well. Jake also saw the look of surprise on her features when his father tucked his hand into the crook of her arm and moved her nearer the guests.

"This is Marlo Mayfield. She is catering our luncheon today and has something special planned for the children. Marlo thought they might like to get acquainted with Hammond Stables on their own." There were murmurs of approval from the adults.

His father was making certain that these people realized that if the next few hours flopped that she, and she alone, was responsible, Jake realized. Then Randall nodded to Marlo as if to say, "You're on."

"I hope you all enjoy scavenger hunts," she addressed the restless children, "because that's what we're doing. I've got the first clue here." Her eyes began to sparkle as she spelled out the details of the game, intent, playful and beautiful all at once.

The oldest boy, who was about fifteen, blurted, "At least it will be better than sitting around." They began to crowd closer to Marlo. The littlest ones reached eagerly for the scraps of paper that she was holding. She quickly formed teams of three. From the corner of his eye, Jake noticed that the men who'd come to talk to Randall were smiling.

"Now you can read your first clue," she told the children.

The fifteen-year-old read aloud. "'Where a horse would go if he wanted to clean up for a party like this one.'"

One of the adults chuckled knowingly.

"I'll bet I know!" a girl with pigtails and pink cutoffs exclaimed. The entire group took off running, searching for the location of the wash stalls.

Marlo turned to the parents. "Some of the clues are harder than others, so it should take a while. The stable hands will watch out for them so no one gets hurt. They can also give helpful hints if everyone is stuck on a clue. The last clue reveals where the picnic table is set up for their lunch. There are prizes there. You probably have an hour and a half of uninterrupted conversation before they all return."

"Brilliant!" one of the men interjected. "I thought this might be a problem with the kids underfoot, but now…" He slapped Randall on the shoulder. "You'd better show us those two-year-olds you've been talking about."

As the others disappeared, Jake hung back and fell into step with Marlo. "I have to give you credit. How did you get the men to agree to help out? They can be a crusty bunch."

She tipped her head to one side in that way he'd observed. It made her appear flirty, although she likely didn't realize it. "I asked them. Nicely, of course. Lucy and I made a special brown-bag lunch for them, as well."

"Bribery. Nice touch." It would be entertaining, he realized, just to watch how this day would unfold. "Now what?"

"I just make sure everything is going smoothly." An earsplitting wail reverberated somewhere inside the barn. "And it looks like we've hit our first bump." Marlo took off for the barn with Jake close behind.

"Don't you have to be with those people?" Marlo asked breathlessly.

"They don't need me, but maybe you'll need my help." *And hopefully not that of an ambulance,* Jake thought to himself.

The kids were clustered in the center aisle, big-eyed and pale.

"What's going on?" Marlo said, with admirable calm in her voice.

"Anna wanted to see what was up those steps." A small boy pointed to a staircase leading up to the hayloft.

"We told her that wasn't where the clue would be, it didn't say anything about stairs or climbing or even hay, but she wanted to see anyway."

"She's so snoopy," an eight- or nine-year-old girl with a blond ponytail said. "She's always getting into trouble."

"She's dumb," a burly ten-year-old added unsympathetically. "She's my sister and she's scared of heights. She knew better than to go up there. Now she can't get down."

Grateful that it didn't appear that bloodshed was involved, Jake headed for the staircase. He reached the loft only seconds ahead of Marlo, who was close on his tail.

"Oh, my," Marlo murmured as they stared up at the vast heaps of small bales set neatly into place, stacked nearly ten feet high. A wooden ladder rested against one of the tall heaps and the little girl clung to the top of the ladder, screaming at the top of her lungs.

"I told you she was dumb," a disgusted voice said behind them. It was the girl's brother, who had climbed the stairs to get a better look at his sister's predicament. "Now what are you going to do, Anna? You're stuck!" Then he added without a hint of brotherly love, "Maybe for life! Wait until I tell Mom and Dad. They'll leave you up there, I'll bet."

The girl's wails intensified. For a brief moment, Jake gave thanks for not having siblings.

Marlo took the boy by the shoulders and gently turned him around so he was facing the stairs. "We'll have her down in a minute. Why don't you wait for us downstairs?"

"A minute? Are you sure?" He sounded dreadfully disappointed. "Bummer."

Meanwhile, Jake moved swiftly to the ladder and climbed it until he was just under the howling child. "You're okay now. I'm right behind you so you can't fall. Just put one foot on the rung below you and I'll walk you down, okay?"

Anna quit howling but continued to snivel as Jake walked her backward off the ladder. When she reached the floor, she wiped the tears from her eyes. Then they narrowed into slits. "Where's my brother? I'm going to pound him."

"She recovered quickly," Marlo said.

"Yes, but her brother might not. I think she's concocting devious plans for the drive home in the back of their parents' car."

"At least they're on to the next clue and not much worse for wear." She ran her fingers through her hair until it stood on end.

"Want some coffee? There's fresh in the break room." He didn't feel like leaving her side. He found it too soothing and too pleasurable to disturb.

"What about the horses and your guests?"

"I believe I'm needed more here—to pick damsels in distress out of haymows. Besides, Dad loves to show the horses. He'd rather have me here, making sure that none of the kids get hurt." And he'd definitely rather be here, Jake thought.

"Suit yourself. I doubt this will be the last of the minor calamities. I could use the help."

Almost as if on cue, they heard a yelp and peals of childish laughter. By the time they reached the paddock, the youngest of the children, a little boy with pale blond hair and huge, horn-rimmed glasses which made him look like a tiny scholar was pulling his foot out of a large, relatively fresh pile of horse droppings. His eyes were huge behind the thick glasses and his lower lip quivered.

"No problem," Marlo announced briskly. She strode to the little boy and picked him out of the muck. "Looks like we'll have to wash *you* off in the wash stall, buddy. What do you think about that?"

The little guy's expression brightened. "Me? Cool!"

Like the Pied Piper, the children followed Marlo to watch the show.

As Jake waited outside, listening to the laughter, and Marlo used a sprayer to banish the grime from the child's foot, he smiled to himself. There hadn't been this much fun on the ranch since…he couldn't remember when. Granted, the stables had always been his retreat, but Marlo added a new element to the place—laughter, lightheartedness and fun. He hadn't realized how much of that was missing until she'd arrived. Now, once that he'd experienced it, he didn't want to let it—or her—go.

By the time Randall and his buyers returned, the game was still going on and excitement for it had built rather than lessened. It went far better than any of them had expected, Jake realized, especially his father, who was downright jolly as the meal the Divas had prepared was served.

As Marlo and Lucy were cleaning up the remnants of the meal, Jake walked into the kitchen. "Whatever you did with those kids, it worked miracles. As Dad showed the horses, the parents watched the children running around and laughing in the distance. The kids were happy but not underfoot. You made the day memorable."

In a positive way, he added to himself. There were so many negative ways the day could have been etched into people's minds, with all these children running around. Fire, stampedes and broken bones came to mind. He found himself genuinely happy that it had all worked out so well, not just for himself, but for Marlo.

"It was actually my father who finally figured out the haddock-paddock connection for the kids," he continued. "If Dad could pat himself on the back for hiring you, I believe he would. In fact, I think we're having a little difficulty getting them to leave. Would you like to come and say goodbye?"

Marlo followed Jake to the front door, where the little boy named Theo, the one who'd had the foot-washing incident, had his arms crossed and lower lip poked out in a pout. "I don't want to go. It's *fun* here."

Randall looked downright jolly as he patted the boy on the head. "Maybe you'll come back with your father sometime. It sounds like we'll be working together often."

Jake gave Marlo two thumbs-ups.

Chapter Twelve

"Your scheme was brilliant," Randall said, approaching Marlo as she cleared away the last debris in the luncheon.

"Sir?" Had she heard correctly?

"Once my clients knew their children were being both entertained and schooled about Hammond Stables, they completely relaxed. They came here planning to invest in one or two horses and are now planning to buy at least four."

"I'm glad." She scuffed her toe in the hard-packed earth. "I admit that I was nervous. I'm relieved the kids didn't think it was an absolute bore."

"You think *you're* glad? In my mind, your idea was a calamity in the making, but my son had faith in you, and it paid off." He stuck out his hand to shake Marlo's. "Thank you." Without another word, he walked off.

"By the look on your face, I'm afraid to think what my father might have said to you." Jake sauntered over, hands in his pocket, sun glinting off his dark hair, that ever-ready smile on his face.

"He thanked and insulted me in the same breath. He called me brilliant and a calamity. I don't know if I should be celebrating or moping."

"Not the latter." Jake looked both sympathetic and amused. "It's best to take Dad with a grain of salt. He's not a very happy man sometimes. He drives himself. I learned a long time ago to relax and go with the flow. I'm a lover not a fighter."

To her surprise, he put his arm around her and nudged her toward the barn. "Come on. I have something to show you."

She didn't try to shrug his arm away. It felt warm, protective and even safe, she realized as she luxuriated in the embrace. For a moment at least, Marlo relished the heavy drape of his arm across her shoulders. Then she began to stew over the attraction she felt toward this man.

He was affectionate toward everyone, Marlo thought. Why, she'd seen him even put his arm around his father when the man was acting like a prickly pear. *He simply doesn't realize how charming and loveable he is because it's his natural state,* she reminded herself. If Lucy were here he'd do the same thing to her. She couldn't blow this brief touch out of proportion. She had to be careful. Her heart wanted to go places that her mind would not allow.

By the time they'd reached the barn, Marlo had talked herself out of believing that Jake's casual embrace meant anything at all. "What's in here?"

"Something I want you to see. We have a mare in labor, and her foal should be born soon. Come." He entwined his fingers in hers and led her to an oversize stall at the back of the barn, where a corpulent black mare with a white blaze and four white feet stood. Her legs were slightly splayed and her breathing audible.

Two men were in the stall with her, one on each side. "Any minute now," one of them murmured. "Apparently, she's not going to lie down. Here it comes…."

Marlo gasped as a spindly legged baby, still wrapped in amniotic membranes, slid from the mother and landed on the straw-matted floor in a squishy thump. Dust motes sprayed into the air and danced in the sunlight filtering through the barn window.

"Is it dead?" she gasped.

"No. Everything is fine." Jake moved toward the foal's head and pulled at bits of the amniotic sac, clearing it away from the baby's nose. The mother butted the baby gently with her head before giving a great, heaving sigh. Knees buckling, she lay down by the infant and began to pull at the membranes with her teeth.

"We'll wait until mama cleans him up," Jake said. "Pretty soon the colt will try to stand. It's quite a sight, a baby that's all legs, on its feet for the first time."

For Marlo, time stopped. She didn't realize she clung to Jake or that he'd tucked her beneath his arm as they stood and leaned his cheek against her hair, or that the men who'd been in the stall with them had slipped away. Her gaze was riveted on the wet, black foal and the ministering mother who seemed to know exactly what to do with this new addition to her life.

"She's going to be a good mother," Jake said softly, almost as if he'd read Marlo's mind. "This is her first colt, and she got right down to business."

"Her first and she knows how, just like that?"

"Nature is a remarkable thing. It is, in fact, what made me believe in the Creator, the Divine Designer. Every birth unfolds like a miracle. You'll never convince me that anything is a complete accident."

And as if to put an exclamation point on what Jake was saying, the colt began to struggle to his feet. His knobby little legs looked like a batch of tangled pickup sticks, but after a few wobbly tries, he got them organized and straightened out. He finally stood, swaying as if there were a gusty wind.

"He's adorable!" Marlo couldn't take her eyes off the soft-eyed baby. "A miracle!"

As if miracles were coming in bunches these day, mama horse, with a great heave, came to her feet, as well. Then, as if it had been orchestrated in heaven itself—which it had, Marlo was to think later—the colt, its nose bumping along its mother's side, found what it was looking for and began to nurse.

"Hey, what's this?" Jake ran a finger along Marlo's cheek and came away with tears.

She snuffled and wiped her nose on her sleeve. "I've never shared anything like that with anyone. It's the most beautiful thing I've ever seen. Thank you."

He smiled at her with that soft, disarming smile that so unnerved her. "Thank you, for reminding me what a miracle birth is. We have so many foals here that sometimes I take it for granted. It's good to see it through your eyes and to remember what an amazing event it really is."

She unconsciously reached out and wound her fingers in the fabric of his sleeve, holding on to him as though she might topple without his presence. She leaned into him then, her gaze still on the nursing foal.

"Marlo, I…" Something in his tone made her look up at him just as he tilted his head down and his soft warm lips grazed her own.

She didn't pull away. She didn't want to. The moment she'd thought was already perfect was made doubly so. She could barely breathe. Her chest was too filled with joy to take more than a short, shallow breath before she exhaled again.

"I'm sorry, Marlo, I didn't mean… I want to tell you…"

She lifted a finger to his lips, not wanting him to mar the moment with words. "We were swept away by a miracle. It's all right." She tipped her head to look at him and he kissed her again. As her eyes fluttered shut, her ever-vigilant mind added, *Just this once.*

Her eyes flew open and, realizing how deeply she was falling under his spell, Marlo pulled away. To accept a kiss was one thing, to divide affections between a couple like Jake and Sabrina was quite another.

She was exceptionally emotional at the moment, she told herself. That was all understandable, having been witness to the miraculous. "What will you name him?"

"Oh, something long and convoluted that refers to his bloodlines, I suppose." Jake kept his arm draped across her shoulders. "We usually refer to the foal's parents' names within its new name. I often tack on a more manageable nickname, as well."

"Like what? Do you have something picked out for this little guy?" Marlo continued to marvel at the enthusiastically nursing colt and its forbearing mother.

"I do. Want to hear it?"

She turned her face up toward his. "Please."

"Marlo's Miracle. Miracle for short. What do you think of that?"

If her heart stopped beating from sheer delight, would it start again? Marlo put her hand to her chest to check. "It's too much."

"Nothing is too much for you." His words were tender. "Marlo's Miracle it is." He looked her over much like he'd studied the colt. "You look like you were actively involved in this birth. I see you have hay in your hair."

Marlo swatted at her head. "Is it gone?"

"Most of it." Gently, he pulled a long bit of straw from somewhere behind her ear.

He began to lower his lips toward hers again when she pulled away. "I don't know how to thank you for this…."

"No thanks needed. This is what I wanted to do. Marlo, I…"

He was interrupted by the sound of a sports car roaring into the yard.

She took the moment to say, "We'd better go outside."

When they emerged from the barn, Sabrina, Alfred and

Cammi were there talking to Randall. Sabrina, her eyes glittering like hard glass, stared at them and focused a daggered stare at Marlo as she and Jake approached.

Then Sabrina turned away, put on a dazzling smile that didn't hint at the silent fury she'd directed at Marlo and sashayed toward Jake.

Knees trembling, Marlo glanced wildly around for Lucy. The Divas van was parked in the driveway of the house and Lucy was just getting in.

"I'd better go now," Marlo murmured to Jake. "I'd call this very bad timing."

Randall chose that moment to stride across the driveway to Jake. "Alfred has a question for you," he said brusquely.

"Later," Jake whispered in her ear, before walking off. When he was out of earshot, Randall turned to Marlo. "My son is charming, but don't let him fool you. His path has been set for a long time. Our family has…plans…for him."

Cheeks flaming, Marlo headed for the van that Lucy already had idling. She jumped in and closed the door as Lucy, seeing Marlo's expression, hit the gas.

"What was that about?" Lucy asked, her eyes large in her head. "Randall Hammond looked very upset."

"He just warned me away from his son. He says the family has 'plans' for him. They obviously don't include me. Little does he know that I'm not after his son."

"Jake's a big boy. He can take care of himself. Besides, you are the last person who would disrupt Randall's 'plan' for Jake and Sabrina to get together. We both know that."

Tears pressed at the back of Marlo's eyes. "Let's go home, Lucy."

Just what she didn't need, Marlo thought as she looked at the day's schedule. Angela had made an appointment to come in to talk about her wedding. After the dustup with Sabrina and Randall at Hammond Stables, Marlo felt sure that the single life was meant for her. There was no way she was going to put herself in a position where she could be the "other woman," no matter how innocently it had come about. What was more, Marlo didn't want to hear Angela's gushing, when all she felt about herself was disgust and dismay. Worse yet, she'd only been apart from Jake for twenty-four hours and she already missed him.

But she and Jake could still be friends, Marlo thought, despite Sabrina's disapproval. She was hardly competition for Sabrina in the beauty department, Marlo thought. There was nothing glamorous about her—she was the cute, dark-haired girl-next-door type. It was almost unearthly how lovely Sabrina was, though her personality left something to be desired. According to the photos she'd seen at Jake's house, his mother and grandmother were also beautiful women. The Hammond men obviously liked trophy wives. The only kind of trophy Marlo knew she could win was a 4-H blue ribbon, or maybe a third-place softball prize.

The bell rang, indicating that Angela had arrived. Before Marlo could go out to greet her, she'd forged her way into the back room, waving a large, white three-ring binder with a photo of her and her fiancé on the cover.

"I've got it all planned and it's going to be wonderful," she announced. "All the Divas have to do is implement it. How are you at making popovers in the shape of hearts? Let's sit down and get started."

Silently, Marlo made a vow to never—ever—work for Angela again on anything bigger than the Bridesmaids' Luncheon. If this didn't go down in history as the most complicated, frustrating, *perfect* wedding in history, she'd eat her socks.

"And I want handmade mints in the shapes of hearts, leaves

and gerbera daisies." Angela tapped the front of her notebook with a Waterman pen that had to have cost well over a hundred bucks. "The hearts will be pink, of course, and take up the center of the plates. Won't that be lovely?"

"A vision," Marlo said wearily.

Lucy, who had been scribbling notes as fast as she could, looked up. "Some of these details—attractive as they are, could add up costwise."

"Expense is no issue," Angle said grandly. "We both want everything to be perfect." She eyed her two friends. "You will have to figure out how to make the catering work while you are both bridesmaids, you know."

"About that," Marlo began, hoping that she could somehow worm her way out of double duty.

"I insist. Hire whoever you must. I can't get married without the two of you in my party, that's all there is to it." Angela tucked the expensive pen into her even more expensive purse. "You two are brilliant. I know you'll figure it out."

And that was that.

After two hours of detailed instructions about everything from the flavor of the wedding cake to the size mushrooms she preferred, Angela skewered Marlo with a sharp look. "You *will* be bringing a date to the wedding, correct?"

Marlo's heart sank. "I'm not sure I can juggle being a bridesmaid, running the kitchen and entertaining a date, Angela. Something would have to be left out, and it would likely be the poor fellow I dragged with me. Maybe I should…"

"I've got the tables planned already. You *must* bring a date, or you will throw everything off." Angela smiled at her and Marlo imagined she could see Bridezilla's fangs. "Put it on your list."

And in a pouf of perfume, she was gone.

Marlo turned to her friend. "Lucy, I just can't... A *date?* Not on top of everything else!"

Lucy held up a hand. "We'll find you someone who doesn't mind entertaining himself to come with you, as a place filler. What's Bryan doing that weekend?"

"Kelly will be home and you know she won't let him out of her sight."

"Then he's out. I've already asked my brother to escort me, or I'd let you have him." Lucy frowned. "Isn't there someone with whom you feel totally comfortable?"

Sure, Marlo thought—but she'd been clearly warned to stay away from him.

Despite her misgivings and reservations, Marlo couldn't steer free of Jake for long.

"Why haven't you been out?" was his first question when Marlo picked up the phone three days later. "We aren't going to have much time to make you comfortable with the animals, once the kids are here."

"I haven't had time, Jake. Maybe I'm not the best one to do this. It's a great program, I'm sure. You should find yourself people who..."

"Care? I want people who feel passionate about this, and I know you do. I can feel it in you. Don't give me the runaround. Come out later today. I'm tying up details, and you're one of my details." His voice softened. "Please?"

"Well, when you put it like that." Marlo was relieved that he approached her as a business detail. Even Sabrina couldn't quibble with that.

Chapter Thirteen

"She's awfully big." Marlo eyed the glistening roan. The mare eyeballed her right back. "I'm not so sure about this, Jake."

"She's small, actually, only about fifteen hands." He leaned casually against the animal, his arm draped against her rump. With his wind-ruffled hair and easy smile, Jake looked as natural and comfortable as if he were lazing in a recliner. Marlo, on the other hand, was developing a nasty sunburn, and her windswept curls felt like she was in a hair-conditioner commercial gone wrong.

Brave in the face of danger, she thought. *Check.*

"It's all relative." She reached out a hand and the horse shifted its weight, eliciting a small squeak from Marlo. "She's mad at me."

"How can you tell? Horses have fixed features. They can't frown." Jake moved nearer and the heady masculine scent of leather and warm horse swirled around her.

Even fearing for her life beneath the hooves of this creature didn't diminish the blissful moment. He stood shoulder-to-shoulder with her, their sleeves brushing. The touch had a rather unfortunate effect on the pounding of her heart.

Then the horse tossed its head and Marlo jumped back.

"Look at her eyes, she's rolling them. She thinks I'm an idiot. I know I agreed to come to the stables and get up close and personal with the horses you're using for the hippotherapy program, but I've reconsidered. I think I'd be better as a receptionist or bookkeeper. My forte is obviously not working with animals." The mare whinnied and both Marlo's feet nearly left the ground.

"She's not upset, she's part Appaloosa."

"As if that explains everything." How much more foolish could she feel about her lack of knowledge?

"She's not part of our breeding program." Jake rubbed the horse's neck with a practiced hand. "Lovey is my mother's personal riding horse. Mom doesn't ride much anymore, and needs a very gentle horse. She's part quarter horse and part Appaloosa." He pointed at the horse's rump. "See those faint white spots in her hair? That and the showing white around her eyes are clues to the Appaloosa portion of her heritage. Lovey is one of those bomb-proof horses I talked about."

"So, if a five-year-old can ride her, then I should be able to brush her without getting trampled?"

"Something like that." Gently, he slipped her fingers through the strap of a curry brush, his touch as calming to her as it was to the horse. "Try it, you'll like it."

Marlo reached out to brush a flank and Lovey swung her back end just out of Marlo's reach.

"Why is she doing that?"

"Because you're nervous."

"Oh, sure, blame me!" She backed up, sat down on a nearby wooden stool and crossed her arms. "Fire me here and now, Jake. I'll be no help to you whatsoever."

Why had she thought she could do this, anyway? Discouraged, she waited for him to send her away.

Instead, he took her hands and tugged her to her feet. Then, standing close beside her, Jake put his hand over hers as she held the curry brush, and guided her gently along the horse's side. "Horses are able to sense and mirror the emotions of their riders and the people around them. Lovey is particularly sensitive. She's feeling your nerves. When you calm down, she will, too."

He seemed to be getting a case of nerves himself, he thought and Marlo was to blame for that. The woman was a riddle—gentle yet strong, savvy yet innocent, cautious yet brave. She got to him in a way that hadn't happened to him often. As he stood between her and Lovey, crooning something unintelligible into the horse's ear, he felt Marlo begin to relax. Tension eased away as they stood and Jake could sense Marlo's shoulders releasing just as Lovey lowered her head. The horse's body shuddered and she gave a contented sigh.

"Hear that?" Jake said. "She's calming down."

"Me, too," Marlo said on her own sigh. "She's a beautiful animal." Lovey turned her head toward Marlo and gave her an affectionate nudge.

"You can ride her if you like. I'll saddle her. We'll take one of the easy trails. Just a walk, no trotting or loping required."

"Can't I just keep doing this? It feels so...safe." Marlo rested her cheek against the horse's smooth neck.

"And I thought you were a risk-taker." He intentionally kept his voice light. She reminded him of a butterfly ready to alight on a branch, but so easily frightened away. "Cammi rides Lovey. I think you'll do as well as an eight-year-old."

"Thanks for the vote of confidence, but I need to work up to it. Is there anything else I could do first to, you know, to get in the mood?"

When she turned those wide blue eyes up at him, he felt a pinch of excitement in his belly.

"Sure." He took the curry comb from her hand. "I've got just the thing."

He led her into the barn and shoved a pitchfork into her hand. "Since you know how to use a curry comb, it's time for this."

Her face crinkled in wrinkled distaste. "If this is your way of convincing me that I should ride, it's not working."

He opened wide a stall door. "I'll get the wheelbarrow. You'll need it to muck out the stall."

"Muck?" Marlo looked more closely at the stall floor. "Oh, I don't think…"

"There are plenty of things you can to do if you don't care to ride," he responded cheerfully. "We certainly have a lot of stalls to clean out. You'd better get busy."

Marlo leaned the pitchfork against the wall and put her hands on her hips. "Wait a minute, buddy, if you think this is going to get me to agree to go riding with you…" a whiff of the interior of the stall hit her nostrils "…you might be right."

"Great." His wide smile revealed that he'd gotten exactly what he'd wanted. "Want to learn how to saddle Lovey? We'll ride western. That will be a good place to start."

"Haven't I learned enough for one day?"

"Education is a wonderful thing. Let me show you the tack room."

Jake carefully chose the bridle and bit, blanket and saddle, that he was sure would be best for her. He wanted no equipment failures the first time he got her on a horse. When they were outside again he said, "Take the blanket, make sure there is nothing like a burr on it. Then throw it over her back. If there's a clump of dirt or a thorn next to her skin it will hurt her and she'll be difficult to control."

Marlo ran the palm of her hand over the blanket. "Now what?"

"Slip it over her. Move slowly and talk to her while you're doing it."

"What should I say?"

"Tell her what a beautiful girl she is and how much you like her."

"That's it?"

"Wouldn't it please you if I told you that?" His voice was soft and low and seemed to caress her, even from a distance.

He saw her skin flush and realized that, though she wasn't about to tell him so, it was possible she could like it very much. Jake smiled to himself.

Carefully, Marlo lifted her arms and slid the thick pad onto Lovey's back. "Nice girl, good girl. What a sweet little lady you are," she crooned. Lovey didn't shy. Instead, one ear quirked slightly, as if she were enjoying the compliments.

"Now the saddle." Jake flipped one fender and stirrup backward so it lay across the saddle seat, and thrust it toward Marlo. "Toss it on her back."

"Toss? Just like that?" She looked doubtfully at the leather contraption.

"Up and over."

Taking the saddle from Jake, Marlo promptly staggered backward under its weight and landed on her backside with the saddle sprawling across her. "You didn't tell me it was so heavy!"

"Now you know." He tried to hide his lack of remorse and his amusement as he lifted the saddle off her so Marlo could scramble to her feet.

"Big help you are," Marlo muttered, but obviously realized that he wasn't going to let it get to him. "No lump of leather is going to get me down."

You could say that again, Jake mused, as he watched her struggle. She was slapped with the flopping fenders and stirrups, and once pitched the saddle across Lovey entirely so it fell to the ground on the other side. It was painful to watch, but the only way she'd truly learn. He'd had to do it himself when he was only a child.

Finally, she stepped back triumphantly. "There! How's that?" She felt a puff of pride at her handiwork.

"Interesting," Jake acknowledged with a smile. "Very interesting, in fact."

Wiping a bead of sweat from her forehead, Marlo stared at him. "Interesting? What does that mean?"

"You must have a lot of confidence in your riding ability, that's all. Not many people like to ride backward. Or were you planning to have Lovey walking in reverse all the way around the trail?"

Marlo turned to stare at the patient, beautiful Lovey, and her eyes widened. Jake did everything in his power not to laugh out loud. The horse was holding her head proudly, even though it must have felt quite strange to have the saddle horn over her rump and the cantle on her withers.

"It's on backward," Marlo moaned. "How did that happen?"

"I'm not sure how you did it," Jake admitted cheerfully, "but it couldn't have been easy."

"The story of my life," Marlo muttered, her face as red as the halter Lovey wore.

"I don't know, let's see." And before he could quash the impulse, he put his arms around her, pulled her close and kissed her. It was a long, tender kiss that surprised even him. He released her quickly, stunned by his own visceral reaction to her.

"Jake, I…" She stumbled backward, a plethora of emotions racing across her features. Delight and dismay seemed to be the primary ones, he thought, and hoped delight would win out.

"You do that very well. Not backward at all," he said cheerfully. "Now let's get this fixed so we can ride."

Marlo watched as he flipped the saddle, tightened the cinch and adjusted the headstall and bit in a few smooth movements. He talked as he worked, defining each piece of tack as he used it. His grandfather Samuel had always told him he was a born teacher. Perhaps that was why he so loved to see children learning what there was to know about riding.

When he was done, he handed her the horse's reins. "You stay here. I'll bring my mount out of the barn." He took a minute, once he was inside the dark fortress of the barn, to take a deep breath. Marlo was getting under his skin and he didn't know how to feel or what to do about it. *Go slowly,* he decided. Something frightened her about their relationship. He'd better hold back and tread very carefully until he knew what was what. Jake chose a huge Tennessee walker and led him into the arena where Marlo was nervously standing with the placid Lovey.

"This is Fine and Dandy. I call her Dandy, for short."

Good kisser. Check.

While Jake expertly saddled the second horse, Marlo's short-circuited brain began to work. He'd kissed her. Again. He shouldn't have done that, she told herself, because… For a moment she couldn't think of a good reason. Oh, yes. Sabrina.

What exactly did it mean to her? She didn't have a lot of time to consider the answer. All she knew was that Jake Hammond was causing her to fall in love with him whether she wanted to or not.

Chapter Fourteen

"Gather your reins in your left hand. It's time to get on." He felt her hand tremble a little beneath his touch as he settled the reins in her hand. Nerves? Something else? Perhaps their kiss had affected her as it had him.

"Always mount on the left side. That's what she's accustomed to."

"Why?" Marlo's voice was thin and uneasy, but she still hadn't lost her curiosity. He liked that in a woman.

"Most horses are trained to be mounted from the left because it is a tradition. Historically, horses were trained that way because a right-handed soldier needed to carry a sword on the left side of his body. That way, he could swing his right leg over the horse without poking the horse with the sword. Lovey is calm enough to mount from either side, but you should always assume that a horse is trained to mount from the left."

"I had no idea this was so complicated."

A little frown creased her forehead and her lips turned down at the corners, which only made Jake want to kiss away the scowl and make her smile again. He reined in his thoughts much as he might an unruly horse. She was jumpy enough, without his alarming her further.

"Put your left leg in the stirrup, and your right hand on the back of the saddle. I find it helps to bounce a bit, to get some momentum, before you push yourself up with your left foot while swinging your right leg over the horse's back."

"You have got to be kidding. That will take more strength and coordination than I have at the moment."

"Untrue. You can do amazing things, Marlo Mayfield, if you'll only try."

That seemed to inspire her. Following his instructions—and with a little shove from behind—she managed to scrabble her way onto the saddle.

She perched there on the powerful horse like a mouse on a keg of dynamite.

Jake slipped the tiny camera he always carried with him to use on job sites from his shirt pocket. "Do you want to commemorate the moment?"

"Does my hair look awful?" Marlo fretted.

"The riding helmet looks wonderful. You're a cross between a jockey and a bowling ball."

"I feel so much better now."

"You'll feel even better when you relax. Lovey isn't going to burst out from under you and run amok, you know. I'll lead you two in circles in a round pen, until you get a feel for each other."

"Actually, I don't know that I will relax. Do you provide a written guarantee?"

"You'll be fine, now that your sense of humor is returning. Let's go out on the trail. You are probably getting dizzy, circling in the round pen, and Lovey has to be bored." He smiled, a dazzling flash of white teeth in stark contrast with his bronzed skin.

"Okay," Marlo said meekly.

He made sure she had the reins properly in her hand before swinging onto his own mount. Jake settled into the saddle like most people might occupy their favorite recliner. When they approached the gate, he leaned over and opened it from the back of his horse.

"Don't try that for yourself yet," he admonished, as he turned Dandy toward the beginning of one of the many riding trails that meandered across the ranch.

"Don't worry," Marlo said through tight lips, as she and Lovey moved out to follow.

She was silent beside him. Jake looked at her to see her jaw rigid and teeth clenched. "Quit gritting your teeth and you'll have a better time. You'll give yourself a headache if you keep doing that."

After ten minutes of tense silence, Marlo took a deep breath. Lovey, Jake knew, had a smooth, easy gait. The horse hadn't even bothered to glance at a rabbit that had crossed the path in front of them.

The rocking motion beneath him was soothing, and the sun on the tops of his thighs loosened his muscles, as he felt himself relaxing into the saddle and stirrups. He had a good idea that the same thing would happen for Marlo, if she'd only give it a chance.

"How are you doing?" Jake matched Dandy's gait to hers. He had a firm grip on the reins. His horse was as explosive as Lovey was gentle, but he enjoyed the test. He'd been riding so long that no horse was much of a challenge anymore, except perhaps something particularly wild and unbroken. Or naturally wary, like Marlo.

"I think I'm beginning to have fun." Marlo's nose was growing pink in the sun and her eyes twinkled. "I know for sure that I'm falling in love with this animal."

"Lovey has that affect on people. Now picture yourself as a child who has spent most of her life in a wheelchair and is enjoying her first ride on a horse."

He watched Marlo as she scanned the horizon. "It feels…" she sought the right word "…free. I feel powerful. I'm visualizing how he would feel up here, on the back of a horse. Like he was flying, I'm sure. There is something about Lovey's serene, patient gait that would make him feel safe, I'm sure of it."

"Him? You've got someone specific in mind?" Jake studied her now-somber face. "You suddenly look very serious. Who are you thinking about?"

She hesitated before responding. "Just about how wonderful this would be for my nephew."

"Bring him out. Have him give it a try."

"I know it would be amazing, but it's not my decision." Then, as if she needed to run from the conversation, she urged Lovey to go a little faster.

Jake caught up to her easily. "I appreciate your passion for my scheme. It's been an uphill climb with my father. It's nice to have someone on my side who believes as I do."

"Sabrina seems to think it's all right," Marlo reminded him.

"So she says." Why did Sabrina always come up when Marlo was around? "I'm sure she'd rather have the attention herself."

"You mean she'd like you to be more interested in her and not spend so much time on this venture?"

"Something like that. Sabrina and Cammi were both raised by doting parents and grandparents. It's going to be a wake-up call when they realize the sun doesn't actually rise and set at their command." He tried to soften the words, but they still sounded harsh. "The fact of the matter was that Alfred spoiled the women in his life too much. It was out of love, of course, but it can be hard to take."

"Cammi is a beautiful child," Marlo pointed out. "I'm sure it's fun to pamper her."

"Her grandfather is one-hundred-percent guilty of that," Jake agreed. "Her parents have had a rocky marriage, and Alfred is her stability. He's practically raised her. I'm very glad they have each other." He shifted restlessly in the saddle, tired of discussing the Dorchesters. "Want to pick up the pace?"

"Ahh…sure." Marlo experimentally leaned forward in the saddle the merest bit, and Lovey obediently moved out.

She might have been screaming, Jake thought, but her internal scream didn't seem to be making it through her lips.

"Hold on," he advised, as he urged Dandy ahead to catch up with her. He searched his mind for something that she could relate to. "This is just like using one of those big exercise balls at the gym. Keep your seat, yet move with the horse."

That, she obviously related to. When Marlo leaned back, Lovey immediately slowed to a plodding walk once again.

"Jake," she asked, as they made their way around one of the many riding trails on Hammond Stables land, "do you know how beautiful this is, or do you see it so often that you take it for granted?" They passed a clear brook on the left, and a stand of maples that eventually would be a glorious cacophony of reds, golds and yellows. A doe stood poised for flight at the edge of the trees, watching them pass, while a hawk turned and wheeled overhead.

"I never take this for granted." His gaze followed her and he saw the doe turn tail and bound into the trees. "Not for a minute. These are my everyday miracles."

"Everyday miracles." She rolled the words across her tongue. "I like that. Miracles don't need to be noisy or spectacular, do they?"

She smiled at him, and the sheer delight in her eyes made him vow to look more closely at maple trees and birds in the future. "God's miracles," she said softly.

Jake nodded. He'd always thought that, even when his father

was grousing about the unsightly weeds growing around a fence post, or when Sabrina was smacking at horseflies and insisting she preferred inside to out. Weeds and horseflies were their own sorts of miracles—not so much to his liking, but miracles nonetheless.

"I like a man who appreciates God's miracles."

He glanced at her sharply. She was still slogging along at his side, gazing at the landscape, seemingly unaware of what she'd just said. The statement hadn't been meant for his ears. Still, it made him smile for the rest of their ride.

When they returned to the round pen an hour later, Jake swung to the ground and handed his reins to a stable hand who appeared out of nowhere. Then he turned to her. "Good job, Marlo! That was excellent for your first time out." He felt like a proud teacher, and he held out his hands as she scrambled off her horse.

"I can do it by myself," she informed him, just before her knees buckled. Jake caught her beneath the arms as she crumpled to the ground, her legs like water.

She felt soft and warm and surprisingly small as she tumbled against his chest. "You'll feel stiff tomorrow, but it's a good stiffness. It will remind you how much fun you had today." He propped her onto her feet, but it took everything in him to release her.

Like a sailor without sea legs, Marlo hobbled to the nearest bench and sat down. "No wonder stereotypical cowboys are always depicted as bowlegged!"

"Take a warm bath tonight and you'll be fine." He plopped down beside her, their outer thighs touching. "Did you have fun?"

"I loved it." Her eyes were shining as she smiled at him. "I know I'm not any good yet, but I'd like to do it some more. It makes me happy."

He hoped so. Personally and inexplicably, he couldn't ever remember being happier.

* * *

"Tell me all about it!" Lucy demanded, when Marlo stopped by Dining with Divas on her way home.

"Later. Bryan's got tickets to the Ordway tonight to see *Phantom,* and I promised I'd go with him." Marlo sampled a bit of the vegetable soup Lucy was preparing.

"You should spend more time dating men of your own choosing, and not babysitting your cousin's boyfriend," Lucy chided. "You should be with men like Jake."

"How many times do I have to tell you Jake and I aren't dating?"

"Then what are you doing?"

"We're friends. Have you got a problem with that?" she said testily.

"Not if you don't. But be careful, Marlo. I don't want to see you hurt."

Marlo drove home to shower and change, but she couldn't wipe Lucy's voice out of her head. *Was* she playing with fire? The bottom line was that she didn't approve of women who moved in on men who were seeing someone else. Her mother had always told her, "Stealing someone's love away from another, no matter how much you care for him, is still stealing." There was no way Marlo wanted to be accused by Sabrina of pilfering Jake's heart. Yet she didn't want to give up spending time with him. She had no choice but to stay on the balance beam and not fall off.

Besides, it wasn't so bad. Things were working well enough. Everyone was happy except Sabrina, who didn't want Marlo anywhere near Jake. Sabrina had nothing to fear from her, whether she knew it or not.

She was relieved to hear her doorbell ring. Her cousin's boyfriend, Bryan, stood in the doorway holding a rose and wearing a foolish grin. Sweetly boyish, Bryan sauntered into Marlo's living room with one hand in his pocket and thrust the rose at her with the other. "Thanks for coming with me tonight. I really didn't want to go alone, and I hated to miss the performance. Kelly is very happy you agreed to join me."

"No problem. It will be fun." She liked Bryan a great deal, and was happy for her cousin. Marlo slipped a short, silver-gray cashmere sweater over her black sheath. "What do you hear from her?"

"She doesn't complain. She worries more about me being bored and lonely than she does about herself."

"Then you've come to the right place. My friend Lucy tells me I need to get out more. Call me anytime."

Bryan's face lit. "I was hoping you'd say that. How do you feel about football? And soccer?"

By the time they reached the theater in St. Paul, Marlo had begun to worry that Kelly's boyfriend could become a full-time job.

They left the car with valet parking and moved with the crowd into the theater lobby.

"We've got plenty of time," Bryan said. "How about a coffee? Ice cream?"

"Sure, why not? I'll wait over there." From the corner of her eye she saw a familiar profile move into view. She would have known that billowing blond hair anywhere. It was Sabrina Dorchester, wearing enough sequins to outfit an entire ballet recital.

A sick feeling washed through Marlo as she looked beyond Sabrina to Jake. He was laughing at something Sabrina had said. The easy companionship between them was apparent. Jake leaned forward and whispered something in her ear and Sabrina lifted a hand to touch his shoulder. The look in her eyes was sheer adoration.

"Here's your coffee." Bryan returned with two paper cups topped with large cookies. "Sorry it took so long. There was a big line… Hey, do you feel okay? You're white as a sheet."

She took the cup with shaking hands. "I just need a little caffeine."

He looked at her, a worried expression on his boyish features. "Don't get sick on me. You're Kelly's favorite cousin, and mine, too."

"I can see why Kelly loves you," Marlo said, forcing a smile.

He flushed to the roots of his sandy hair. "Family is family, Marlo. If you ever need my help, you've got it. Okay?"

"Okay," she whispered. She refused to let the visceral reaction she'd had at seeing Jake and Sabrina together ruin her evening. Instead, she took a bite of the cookie.

They flooded in with the rest of the waiting patrons eager to find their seats, and much to her relief, Marlo lost sight of Jake and Sabrina.

If the play had been *Phantom of the Opera Meets Les Misérables and The Lion King at South Pacific,* it still wouldn't have held her attention. Whatever dialogue was happening onstage was nothing, compared with the discourse going on in her head.

At church on Sunday, the pastor had spoken on the Ten Commandments. Now a single commandment kept rolling through her mind like a catchy, repetitive jingle that gets stuck in one's head. It was the one about not coveting one's neighbor's house, wife, slave, ox, donkey—or anything else that belonged to a neighbor.

I'm sorry, Lord, she thought, feeling the desperate urge to pray. Wanting someone else's almost-fiancé was included in that commandment somewhere. She prayed that He help her to put her relationship with Jake into a healthy perspective. She didn't want her foolishness to jeopardize her work for his hippotherapy program. She needed to focus on what was really important.

And when she wasn't talking to God, she was talking to herself.

She had to control her feelings and back off. Jake was not hers to fawn over or to love. From now on, Lucy could meet with Jake about the events they catered for Hammond Farms. She could hire someone to serve in those occasions in her place.

But what about when she was at the stables? And why was Jake so friendly to her, if he and Sabrina were, as Sabrina hinted, practically married? A stabbing, disconcerting thought came to her. Maybe Jake's talk about God was for *her* benefit, not his own. Maybe he wasn't the kind of man she thought he was.

The idea made her so uncomfortable that she squirmed miserably in her seat until Bryan turned to stare at her. Guiltily, she turned her eyes to the stage, even though what was transpiring there was barely registering. Even the Phantom himself couldn't distract her.

It was all because Angela was getting married that she was panicked at the idea of being the only single woman in her group. She hardly knew the man! She didn't even know Jake's favorite color—unless it was red. So many things in his home were red. She had no idea about his favorite food…but it was avocado. He'd told her the night of the party. And of course she didn't know his jacket size or how he drank his coffee. What had she been thinking?

But she did know those things, she realized suddenly. Size forty-two long. She'd seen his jacket hanging over the back of a kitchen chair. And he preferred his coffee black.

How had that happened? She hadn't even known her last boyfriend's favorite color or jacket size, and they'd dated for several months.

She drooped deeper into the velvety theater seat. She was sunk, truly sunk. She'd fallen for Jake.

There was really only one thing she could do, Marlo realized. She would hide her feelings away until they withered and died.

It was the only logical thing to do. But when had she ever been logical?

At intermission, Bryan wanted to go to the lobby. "This is the best production I've ever seen. And the voices! I want to buy a CD and a T-shirt to send to Kelly. That way she won't feel so left out."

"You go ahead. I'll wait here." She didn't want to risk running into Jake and Sabrina again.

"I'd like you to come with me." Bryan frowned. "Who are you trying to avoid out there?"

"What makes you think I'm trying to avoid anyone? Can't I just sit here and people-watch?"

"I saw it in your expression. There was someone in the lobby you didn't want to see. Is that why you're refusing to go with me now?"

She wasn't quick enough to come up with an answer. She hadn't expected Bryan's words to hit so close to home.

He crossed his arms over his chest. "I'm right, aren't I?"

She sank low in her seat. "Just a flame that hasn't completely died down yet, that's all. The woman he's with told me they're getting married." She didn't mention the pathetic, old-maid complex she'd developed after Angela announced her upcoming marriage. That would be too pitiable, even for sweet, understanding Bryan.

"So? That's no reason to hide, unless… He's hurt you somehow, hasn't he? Was he leading you on while engaged to her?"

He checked the accuracy of his guess on Marlo's responsive features. "That's it, isn't it?"

"That's pretty much it, in a nutshell."

"Come with me, Marlo," Bryan pleaded. "Don't let a guy hurt

you like that. Hold your head up. You may not be with him, but you're with *me!*"

She looked at his handsome, boyish features and sweet smile. Laughing finally, she relented. "Okay. Lead on."

They'd inched their way through the crowd, including a string of ladies lined up for the restroom, and managed to purchase the gifts for Kelly, before Marlo caught sight of Jake. He was standing outside the front door, cell phone to his ear. Sabrina was waiting just inside, looking impatient.

Feeling her stiffen, Bryan glanced up to see where Marlo's gaze was fixed, and whistled softly through his teeth.

Even he was not immune to Sabrina's beauty. "Quick, let's get back to our seats," Marlo pleaded. She didn't want to be seen by Jake and Sabrina, not if she could help it.

"Not quite yet," Bryan said cheerfully. "I'd like to meet your friends."

"Bryan!"

It was too late. Jake was no longer on the phone. He'd re-entered the building, spotted them and was towing a reluctant Sabrina in their direction.

"Hey, Marlo! I didn't know you'd be here. How do you like the production?" As he spoke, Jake looked Bryan over as if he were appraising a piece of horseflesh. Bryan did the same, only studying Jake as if he were an unpleasant bug under a micro-scope.

"Jake, Sabrina, I'd like you to meet my friend Bryan. He's my—" She was about to say "cousin's fiancé" when Bryan smoothly interrupted.

"Nice to meet you." He thrust out his hand to Jake and gave Sabrina an engaging, high-wattage smile that made her blink. Then he shocked Marlo by putting a warm, protective arm around her shoulders. "Any friends of Marlo's are friends of mine."

It was Jake's turn to look surprised. "I didn't realize you were seeing any—"

Sabrina tugged on Jake's sleeve. "The lights are flickering, darling. They're calling us back into the theater."

Bryan gave Marlo a little hug. "Come on, pookie, we'd better get in, too." And before she could say anything, Bryan propelled her toward their entrance, leaving Jake and Sabrina to watch them go.

When they got to their seats, Marlo turned to him and hissed, "*Pookie?* Where did *that* come from?"

"That's what Kelly calls me. It was all I could think of. Sorry. But I saw the look on your face. Listen, Marlo, I'm marrying your cousin, and she's more like you than you might think. I can read a situation. That guy needs to see that you're a desirable woman, not the Gloomy Gertrude you were a few minutes ago." Bryan grinned naughtily. "Now you're interesting. Compelling. Taken."

She had to give him credit. It might not have been the smoothest way out of the awkward situation, but it wasn't bad. Marlo put her hand on Bryan's elbow. "Thanks for being so perceptive. My cousin is one lucky woman."

"You're welcome, pookie."

Chapter Fifteen

Marlo had been in a funk that she hadn't been able to shake since she'd seen Jake and Sabrina at the theater. Even work didn't seem to help, though every time the phone rang, she hoped it was Jake. Finally, her prayers were answered.

"Ms. Mayfield. My name is Julie Frank. I'm Mr. Jake Hammond's secretary. He asked me to give you the schedule for the hippotherapy events at Hammond Stables this week, in case you're free and would like to volunteer." She rattled off a series of days and times so quickly that Marlo barely was able to scratch them down on the unwaxed side of a scrap of freezer paper. "If you have questions you may call me any time between the hours of eight and five at this number."

After she hung up, Marlo stared at the scribbled notes she'd taken. Only last week, Jake would have picked up the phone and called her himself. Now his secretary was their go-between. She felt twinges of both sadness and relief. Jake, too, after meeting Bryan, must have recognized the need for boundaries between them. The relief stemmed from knowing this was the right thing to do. The sadness came from the sense of loss she felt. "Sometimes, Marlo, doing the right thing means doing the hard thing," Aunt Tildy used to say.

Can take a hint. Check.

"What was that about?" Lucy asked. "You look like you are about to burst into tears."

"Nothing much. Jake's secretary just gave me the schedule for the hippotherapy sessions. I'll run out there after work and see what I can do to make myself useful." She thought about what might have been if Sabrina hadn't been in the picture.

Lucy responded as if she'd been reading Marlo's thoughts. "It's Jake and Sabrina, isn't it? You're staying clear of him because of her. Not every woman is as upstanding as you. If they were, the words *the other woman* wouldn't exist."

"You don't have to remind me—of all people—of that. It's reprehensible to step into the lives of a couple and to try to break them apart." It was the wound on her heart left by Jeremiah and company.

"You're special, Marlo, a person others can trust. It's an old-fashioned word, but you are *honorable.*" Lucy's expression grew soft. "I'm grateful that you are my friend."

Marlo threw her arms around Lucy and hugged her as hard as she could. *Honorable* wasn't the word she would use to describe herself. *Obedient,* perhaps—obedient to God's word whether she liked it or not. She didn't have to enjoy what was required of her. She only had to have the faith to know that His will would work out best in the end.

Marlo felt some of her old vitality returning. "At least I can still help with the children and the horses. In the scheme of things, that's what really matters."

"Speaking of children, how's Brady?"

"Overprotected, sheltered, wrapped in cotton batting and, of course, the sweetest boy on the planet. I stopped there this morning. Brady and his dad were playing ball on the front lawn.

Brady hasn't mastered catching yet and Jenny stood on the steps worrying that he'd get hit in the head. She doesn't even trust Brady's own father to toss him a ball."

Her sister was on a path that was going to make Brady into everything she'd feared he might be—timid, easily frightened, totally cognizant of his limits and unaware of his strengths. It was agony to watch what was happening between her sister and her nephew, but she was helpless to stop it.

"Have you been praying about it?" Lucy asked.

"Nonstop."

"Have you been expecting an answer? Sometimes I pray and later realize that on some level I don't expect God to answer," Lucy admitted candidly. "I trust Him enough to pray, but not enough to expect results. Maybe it's an issue I've prayed about so much that it becomes rote, a habit or repetitive mouth prayer, not a heart prayer."

"Ask and expect," Marlo murmured. Lucy was right. She'd prayed for Brady but never quite shrugged off the blanket of helplessness she felt about him. *Expect God to answer.* "Good reminder, Lucy. Thank you. You can read me like a book."

"Yeah," Lucy said cheerfully and stood to get on with her work. "It's too bad that most of the book is written in Chinese."

Hammond Stables was buzzing with activity when Marlo arrived. A trailer was being loaded with show horses and cars were parked willy-nilly near the building which now housed Jake's program. There were mothers and children milling about.

Out of the corner of her eye, Marlo saw the flash of a black riding jacket. Then she was nearly knocked to the ground by Cammi flinging herself toward Marlo's midsection.

"Hi, Marlo! I've been waiting for you to come."

At least someone was eager to see her. The little girl was at the stables nearly every time Marlo was, and a remarkable comradeship had developed between them. Marlo remembered Jake's comment about Cammi's tumultuous home life and had made a special effort with the child. "Hello, Cammi. I love your enthusiasm, but one of these days, if you keep doing that, we'll both bite the dust."

Cammi bounced excitedly on the tips of her toes. Even though she looked like Sabrina, her disposition was quite the opposite of that of her aunt, who Marlo had rarely seen smile, except at Jake.

"Grandpa bought me a new horse. Her name is Feather. Today is the first day I get to ride her. I want you to watch me."

"The very first day?"

Cammi wrinkled her nose. "I wanted to ride the day Feather came, but Mom said I couldn't because I had a bad headache and was throwing up. Ugh."

"How do you feel now?"

"Good." Cammi grabbed her hand. "Come, let me show you."

Marlo wasn't quite sure how it had happened, but Cammi had decided to adopt Marlo into the fold in a way that her aunt Sabrina probably despised. When the little girl wasn't imperious or being spoiled, but acting like the child that she was, she was quite delightful.

"What are all those children waiting around for? Surely they can't all be scheduled to ride."

Cammi flipped her sun-lit curls. "Nah. They're just brothers and sisters hanging around till the rider gets done." She tugged at Marlo's hand. "Come on! You aren't walking fast enough."

Marlo allowed herself to be pulled to a quiet spot between two barns, where Cammi's grandfather, Alfred, was saddling a beautiful black horse that stood patiently under his ministrations. Randall appeared to be supervising.

"Isn't she bee-oo-ti-ful?" Cammi crowed. "I love her so much."

Randall looked up and scowled at Marlo. "Can you do something about the congestion by the office? It's upsetting the horses. Cars and kids everywhere. We can't get a thing done."

To Marlo, it looked like plenty was getting done, but who was she to judge. She squeezed Cammi's hand. "I'll be back in a minute, honey. You get to know Feather, and then I'll watch you ride."

Marlo hurried toward the gaggle of women and children to whom Randall was referring. It could have been a cluster of soccer moms waiting for a game to start, all chatting excitedly. When Marlo neared, they waved her into the group.

"Have you got a child here?" one mother asked Marlo.

"No. I'm a volunteer. Is everything going well for you so far?"

"We're thrilled to be here, all of us. We're having a hard time keeping our other children busy, that's all. That man over there—" the young mother gestured toward Randall "—has been glaring at us all morning. It's just that the kids are restless…and a little bit jealous because they don't get to ride, too. Most of them don't understand why they can't. I suppose the best thing to do is leave them at home, but that's not always possible." The woman smiled at Marlo. "I'm Ellen, by the way."

"I can pop a movie into the DVD player, so the children will have something to do," Marlo offered. "Then, let me think about it and talk to Jake Hammond himself. Perhaps we can come up with something." She paused to smile at the woman. "Thanks for telling me. I know Jake wants this program to be good for everyone involved."

"He must be a great man," Ellen murmured. "This is hugely important to us."

"Handsome, too," another mother said. "He's single, isn't he? Quite a catch."

"Yes, I suppose so," Marlo said vaguely. Not her catch, however. She'd pulled her fishing pole out of the water.

After she'd corralled the kids in the office with a video, and made sure all the mothers knew where the coffeepot was, she returned to Cammi and Feather.

As she passed one of the sheds on the way back to Cammi, she heard Alfred and Randall deep in discussion.

"You can't force Jake into anything, Randall, you never have," Alfred was saying. "He's laid-back, but he has a stubborn streak a mile wide when you push him."

"Obstinate and pigheaded, that's what he can be," Randall growled. "Sabrina can't wait forever…."

"He came by it naturally, Randall. He got it from you."

Then they saw Marlo and stopped talking. The same old discussion was still raging, she deduced.

Randall eyed her as she approached. "What did you do with them? Lock them in a barn?"

"Just diverted them a little. I'm afraid that you'll always have a group of children here while the others are riding. Parents can't necessarily afford to hire babysitters and leave them at home."

"Well, I'm certainly not going to be responsible for babysitting them!" Randall eyed Marlo. "Unless you have an idea. It seems like you are a creative thinker."

A compliment from Randall Hammond? Marlo felt like checking her ears to see if something was wrong with them.

"I do have one that I could talk to Jake about." It had come to her as she'd watched the children gaze enviously at their siblings astride the horses.

"Maybe you'd better tell me first," Randall said. "My son would spend the moon and stars to make this thing work. In this case, I have to be the one with the good financial head."

No, you just want to take back the control you think you're losing, Marlo thought. *Maybe this time it will work out in the program's favor.*

"I was thinking that something like a My Own Pony program might work."

"What's that?"

"I'm not completely sure, because I just made it up," Marlo admitted, "but if there were a couple ponies available for the siblings to groom and pet, they might not be so jealous. It would keep them out from under everyone else's feet, too. I don't know much about horses, but Jake did show me the basics of using a curry comb. If all those children tended to the young horses, you'd have the most well-groomed creatures on the planet." Marlo bit her lip, hoping she hadn't said too much or sounded too en-thusiastic—particularly since she was making this up on the fly.

To her shock and amazement, Alfred said, "I like it, Randall! What better way to introduce kids to horses? Who knows? You might even sell a few riding horses if the kids go home and talk about it enough. I don't think it could hurt your business."

"It sounds like a lot of busy work," Randall grumbled.

"Not so much," Alfred cajoled. "Why, I'll bet Marlo could handle it with one hand tied behind her back."

"So you'd arrange and run it then?" Randall asked, studying Marlo through narrowed eyes.

How had this happened? Marlo's mouth went dry. "I just suggested it. I didn't say I knew what I was doing…"

"Well, you'll do. I watched you handle the party we had here. You're clever. Besides, you're a volunteer. Will you volunteer to set up this My Own Pony thing? I'd appreciate it if you'd keep those kids occupied."

How did one turn down Randall Hammond? Marlo was sure it didn't happen often, and she wasn't about to find out the con-sequences of doing so.

"Sure," she responded. "You do realize that I don't know what I'm doing, don't you?"

Randall looked as if he were fully aware of Marlo's inadequacies, but had decided to move forward nonetheless. "You might as well start today."

Like a marionette with her strings under Randall's control, she bobbed her head in agreement. Here she was again, backing into something she knew nothing about.

Though she knew it at her core, she didn't admit that the real reason she agreed to Randall's demand was that it would allow her to be more deeply involved in the program that was so close to Jake's heart—and to Jake himself.

Chapter Sixteen

"See me ride, Marlo, see me ride!" Cammi, her back straight and her posture relaxed, looked as though she and Feather had been together forever.

"I wish I could ride like that," Marlo muttered to herself, not expecting to be overheard.

Alfred, however, turned his head. "Jake taught her himself. He's an excellent rider. When Sabrina was Cammi's age, he taught her, too." He smiled at the memory. "Jake was a good-looking guy, even as a teenager. Sabrina was completely infatuated with him. I'm glad they've maintained their relationship all these years."

Marlo wasn't nearly so delighted. She wished a guy like Jake were available once in a while, but, in her experience, they were always taken. It was impressive, however, to know what an excellent teacher he was. *Good with children.* She'd have to remember to add that to the List.

"I have something to discuss with Randall. I'll send someone right over to help Cammi off her horse." Alfred started off. "Watch her for a moment, will you?"

As the two men left, Marlo walked toward the fence to observe Cammi. She tried to imagine Jake as a handsome teenager teaching an impressionable young girl to ride. No wonder Sabrina was so possessive about Jake. She'd had him in her corner her entire life.

At least she hadn't made a total fool of herself to Jake before she woke up to the situation, Marlo thought. That was the saving grace. She'd avoided public humiliation. All her torment was private. Only Lucy had an inkling of her feelings. Stoically, Marlo forced a smile to her face and waved at Cammi.

She didn't sense that Jake was behind her until he cleared his throat and stepped up to the fence, his shoulder lightly brushing hers. Jake's presence made her emotions turn traitorous, making her feel things she didn't want to feel.

"She's a good little rider, isn't she?"

"Amazing, even to an inexperienced eye like mine. You did a good job."

"Did Alfred tell you that I gave her lessons?"

"He said you taught Sabrina, too."

Jake didn't take the bait. "I want to teach you, too. You're gentle, patient and firm. I believe you'll have a light touch on the reins, too. What do you think?"

It was a heady idea, considering that Jake chose to teach only the most special of females. Heroically, she resisted the urge.

"I'd better keep my feet on the ground for now. I have a new project around here that will take all my time."

"New project? One I haven't heard about?"

"Actually, it just came up today, in the past hour." She wished he wasn't so enticing. Even his cologne was yummy. *Smells good. Check.* "Your father and I discussed it and he asked me to set it up."

Jake's eyebrows nearly buried themselves in his hairline. "My father? Since when did he become interested in helping me with this?"

"He was upset. There were children, mostly bored siblings of the riders, running in the yard, making noise and getting in the way. I turned on a television, but it loses some of its appeal on a beautiful day like this one."

"I should have known—a self-serving idea. He really hates chaos." Jake sighed. "Spill the beans, what is Dad up to?" He didn't sound as if he expected it to be good.

"I suggested he provide a couple of young horses for the extra children to groom. That way they will be busy and involved with animals, too. My idea was to call it My Own Pony. He liked it, that's all." She grimaced. "And he said that since I was already a volunteer, I might as well volunteer to set it up."

Jake burst out laughing, a delighted and delightful sound. "It's a great idea, Marlo. I wish I'd thought of it myself. My father obviously jumped on it because he realized that you were onto something." He put one foot on the bottom rail of the fence, tipped back the cowboy hat that Marlo had seen him wear occasionally and stared out at the rolling pasture. "I can see it now. My Own Pony. Excellent, really excellent."

He gave her a smile that could have melted sand into glass. "You are very clever, Marlo."

She felt like clamping her hands over her head to keep him from tampering any more with her brain. Jake was dangerous. He could read the phone book aloud to her and still sound like he was flirting.

"All around Jill-of-all-trades, cook, babysitter, pony person, that's me," she said, keeping her tone light.

Before he could respond, Cammi yelled out, "Can you see me ride, Jake? Feather and I are good, aren't we?" She and Feather were doing large circles in the paddock.

"The best, sweetheart. Do you want to get off now? Your grandfather sent me to get you."

"Not yet. This is fun!" The pair moved around the ring almost as one entity.

It was quite lovely to behold, Marlo thought. "That's an amazing horse. It's almost as if it reads Cammi's mind."

"Alfred wouldn't put Cammi on anything but the best. Feather is as well trained as they come."

"Cammi is hard not to love—unless she's in her pouty-princess routine."

Jake smiled. "She's just imitating her aunt, when Sabrina is on her high horse about something. Nothing we—I—can't handle."

Obviously. Marlo stared straight ahead, afraid to look at him, fearful that he could read in her eyes what was happening to her heart.

Then Feather's easy gait faltered. She came to a stop and remained so still that she might have been carved from stone. And as they watched in horror, Cammi drooped forward over the pommel of her English saddle and slumped against the horse's neck. As if in slow motion, she slid sideways, a tangle of arms and legs, and tumbled awkwardly to the ground. Feather, feet planted firmly, didn't flinch or shy away.

"Wha…" Jake swung his leg over the fence and hit the ground running. He was already to Cammi before Marlo could take in what had happened. Large and broad-shouldered, he loomed over the tiny heap on the ground. He turned back and yelled, "Call 911 and get Alfred!"

Marlo dug in her pocket for her cell phone and dialed. Almost as if she'd willed them to appear, Alfred and Randall strolled out of the big house and started walking toward the barn.

"Alfred!" she screamed.

Something in her tone must have sounded an alarm in Alfred's mind, because he broke into a run. He was breathing hard by the time he reached Marlo. "What's wrong?"

She pointed to the spot where Feather stood and Jake bent over the prone form of Cammi. "She just crumpled in the saddle. Feather sensed something was wrong and came to a stop. Then she slid off the horse and onto the ground."

"No…Cammi…" Alfred's voice broke and he scrambled over the fence almost as quickly as Jake had.

By this time Randall had caught up. "What's going on?" he demanded.

"I don't know." Marlo's heart was in her throat as she watched Jake stroke the little girl's hair as she lay on the ground. "It looked like Cammi fainted midride. The horse stopped and hasn't moved since."

She was surprised that neither of the men made an effort to pick Cammi up until she realized that moving her could do more harm than good. These men had obviously seen far more falls from horses than she, and knew what to do, she told herself. The pounding of her heart hammered in her ears as she waited helplessly for something to happen.

"A horse stepping on her could have snapped a bone in half," Randall muttered grimly. "If anything happens to that child it will kill Alfred. You're sure the horse didn't act up?"

"Positive. In fact, it seemed to sense that Cammi was in trouble." She described how Feather had behaved, as best she could. The answer seemed to please Randall.

Already, Marlo could hear a faint siren wailing in the distance. Not only that, the mothers and children in the yard were beginning to walk with the therapy volunteers toward the commotion. Without thinking further, Marlo ran toward them to wave the casual spectators away from the scene. It wouldn't help the hippotherapy program if the participants saw a child on the ground. Even if it wasn't the horse's fault, the broken body of a tiny girl on the hard-packed dirt was an image they wouldn't forget.

Marlo held them at bay until Jake strode up behind her.

"Get in the car," he ordered Marlo, as the EMTs loaded the stretcher and tiny prone figure into the ambulance. "Alfred and Dad are riding with Cammi. We'll follow."

Marlo scrambled into the plush leather interior of the SUV and buckled her seat belt. The grim set of Jake's jaw told her that whatever had happened was serious.

"Is she going to be okay?" Marlo ventured.

"I don't know," he said frankly. "I've never seen anything quite like it." He looked at her, his dark eyes intense. "Time to start praying, Marlo."

She put her hand over his. "I've already started."

By the time they reached the hospital and parked Jake's car, Randall was already in the E.R. waiting room, pacing.

"How is she?" Jake asked.

"I don't know. I haven't heard a thing." He furrowed his eyebrows and stared at Marlo. "You're sure this wasn't Feather's fault?"

"Positive." Marlo reiterated what she had seen.

When she was done and Jake had concurred, Randall's shoulders sagged in relief. "I was the one who helped Alfred choose Feather for Cammi. I'd never forgive myself if something had gone wrong with the horse and it had dumped her."

"It wasn't like that at all, sir." A memory flickered in Marlo's mind. "Did Cammi tell you that she couldn't ride Feather the past couple days because she wasn't feeling well? She told me she'd had a headache and was throwing up. Maybe this episode happened because she was weak or not fully recovered."

What if the horse hadn't been so well trained? What if Cammi had landed roughly? What if she hadn't been wearing a helmet? Marlo shivered at the thoughts. Jake, seeing her tremble, led her to some uncomfortable plastic chairs and made her sit down. Then he sat beside her and wrapped his arm around her shoulder. It was her life raft in a chaotic sea. Eventually the quaking subsided, and Marlo, drained by tension, allowed her head to rest against his shoulder. Comfort. Consolation. Jake.

Marlo closed her eyes and leaned into the strength and steadiness Jake radiated. She opened them again when Alfred, looking exhausted and years older than he had at the ranch, entered the waiting room.

"Cammi has had a stroke," Alfred said, his voice filled with disbelief. "How can a child have a stroke? That's for the elderly, like me. Why couldn't it have been me?"

Randall paled beneath his tan and sat down hard.

"They've got to be wrong," Alfred continued in a flat voice. "Don't they?"

At that moment a woman in a white jacket walked into the room and studied the foursome.

"Cammi's family?" she inquired. Both Randall and Alfred nodded.

"My name is Dr. Erica Jacobs." She looked at her clipboard. "Have Cammi's parents been notified that she's in the hospital?"

"Most of my family members are out of town for a wedding," Alfred said. "I've tried to reach them, but they have no doubt turned off their cell phones during the ceremony. Cammi's mother will call later tonight, I'm sure."

"Very well. As you heard in the E.R., Mr. Dorchester, Cammi has suffered a stroke. That's unusual in children, and happens to only about two to six in one hundred thousand. There are multiple causes, but we've ruled out infection and trauma. Other things we'll look for are congenital or acquired heart disease. It may be related to a heart condition that's gone undetected until now. That's a common cause. It's unlikely that it's an intracranial tumor...."

Alfred groaned and put his head into his hands.

The doctor gave the little group a compassionate look. "The news is actually quite good. There are no seizures or eye-movement problems. Children often recover better than adults. Perhaps that is because of the immaturity of the brain. It has the ability to repair itself and to adapt. The other good news is that you got her to the hospital right away, so we could begin applying neuroprotective measures."

"She told me she'd had a headache the past couple days," Marlo blurted into the stunned silence that ensued.

The doctor nodded. "That makes sense. A headache is often an early sign of stroke. She has weakness on one side of her body and a slight slurring of words. We'll keep her in the hospital and then in rehabilitation as long as we need to. She's in good hands." The doctor smiled sympathetically. "I know this has been a shock, but let's wait a bit before we jump to any conclusions. I'm very optimistic about her prognosis."

After the doctor left, Alfred murmured, "'Weakness?' What if it doesn't go away? What if she's paralyzed?"

"Don't go there, Alfred," Randall said sharply. He stood and took charge.

"Come. We'll find which room she'll be in."

When they were gone, Jake expelled a long breath. "Poor kid. I hope she's okay." Then he added grimly, "Dad doesn't know it yet, but before this is done he may be *very* happy that Hammond Stables is in the horse-therapy business."

He reached for Marlo and she stepped into his arms for comfort, knowing that Jake's pain was much worse than her own. He'd known the little girl her entire life. Marlo had only loved her for a little while. They stayed that way a long time, Marlo's head against his chest, listening to his strong and steady heartbeat. She felt as if she'd come home.

"I suppose I should take you back to Hammond Stables to get your car," Jake said reluctantly.

"It's okay. Not yet. I'm sure I'd just pace the floor at home."

"Want to get some coffee? There's a coffee shop a couple blocks from here," Jake suggested.

"Sure."

The coffee shop was empty, except for a businessman whose nose was buried deep in a newspaper. They took a booth in the far corner from the cash register after Jake bought two oversize muffins brimming with nuts and coconut and two mugs of the darkest, richest brew.

Wordlessly, they ate the muffins and then sat silently staring deep into the bottoms of their mugs.

After a few minutes of complete silence, out of the blue, Jake inquired, "How did you like the play?"

"Huh? Oh, fine, I guess." Marlo could hardly remember what he was asking about. Cammi's situation made today feel like a transition into a whole new century.

"Nice-looking guy you were with," Jake said casually.

Was he making polite conversation or did he actually care? Marlo decided it was less embarrassing to play along than to explain about her cousin and about Bryan's gentlemanly instinct to protect her from a man he perceived to be a lothario. "Yes. He is."

"Known him long?"

"Years. We went to school together." She'd been the one to introduce Bryan to her cousin Kelly, in fact.

"Have you seen many plays together?" Jake just wouldn't let it go.

"That was the first actually." Restlessly, she turned the mug between the palms of her hands

"What do you do when you're together, if you don't mind my asking? Sports? Movies?"

His piercing look made Marlo feel as if she was being run through a CAT scan.

"We hang out at my cousin's house mostly."

"Watching movies?"

"Croquet, actually." She grinned at the puzzled expression on his face. "I swing a pretty mean mallet."

"Sounds like fun."

The man almost sounded wistful, Marlo realized, or…could it be? Jealous? Surely not. What was there to be jealous about? Then it struck her. It was about Bryan! All that questioning made Jake sound jealous of Bryan.

Marlo didn't know whether to laugh or cry. All she did know is that she needed to finally find out the truth about him and Sabrina.

"Jake, exactly what is your relationship with—" She was about to say "Sabrina" when his cell phone rang, "The William Tell Overture," of all things.

He fished into his pocket to find it. "Jake, here. Oh, hi, Nick, what's up?" He listened intently for a long moment. "The vet is on the way? Good. I'll be there as soon as I can."

When he looked back at her he was frowning. "We have a horse down, one of our stallions. I need to get back to the stables ASAP."

"Let's go. I'll pick up my car there and go home."

He nodded absently, his mind already a million miles away from the conversation she'd begun. Another time, perhaps, they could finish what she'd started, but Marlo had a hunch it wouldn't be in the near future.

Chapter Seventeen

"Gently, very gently. That's right. You don't like to have your hair combed the wrong way, do you? Neither does Frankie." The child standing between Marlo and the rotund belly of a little paint giggled. She and a little boy almost as chunky as the pony in question were in the round pen, finishing up the last of Frankie's many grooming sessions for the day. All morning, children had clamored to brush the ponies Hammond Stables provided for the My Own Pony crowd.

Jake, who'd been observing, leaned heavily on the top rail of a nearby fence and stared across the rolling pastures to the horizon beyond. His riding boot was wedged between the fence rails, and his neat Stetson was tilted back on his thick, dark hair. Fall was in the air and the trees were modeling their flashiest colors, reds, oranges and yellows.

"Hey." She wandered toward him.

"Hey, yourself." He turned to look at her and smiled faintly. She hadn't seen much of him lately, since he'd been, as he put it, "Putting out fires on all fronts"—the stables, the architectural firm and the absence of his father from the business. Randall was spending a lot of time with Alfred these days, who was at the hospital with Cammi. "The kids and their mothers love My Own Pony. It was a stroke of genius, Marlo."

"I love it, too. It's given me a chance to learn about horses at my own speed. I can actually put a saddle on in the right direction now."

A slow, lazy smile spread across his features and his eyes began to twinkle. "That's progress, but I must admit I enjoyed seeing the expression on your face after you realized you'd put that saddle on backward. Which reminds me, how are those minis working out?" He'd arrived a few days ago, pulling a trailer with a pair of adorable miniature horses inside, and the kids had gone wild.

She moved to the fence and thrust her own boot—her first purchase after she'd started here—between the rails and imitated his stance. "Perfectly. They're ideal for the smaller children. They can learn everything about grooming and caring for a horse that's just their size. Even I have learned how to pick feet and groom manes and tails. It's less intimidating when you can look *down* on the horse."

He turned slowly until he was facing her, his arm still resting on the fence rail. "Marlo, I don't know how to thank you. You've been more help than I ever expected or imagined, especially during Cammi's illness."

She'd been part-time receptionist, My Own Pony volunteer and cleaning lady in recent days. She'd led horses in the arena for the therapists, walked fussy babies for harried mothers and still managed to keep up with the Dining with Divas schedule, thanks to Lucy, who'd taken on more in the prep kitchen.

And she would have done even more, if she could have. Jake and Cammi had taken over most of her thoughts.

"Cammi loves the fact that you've visited her every day. Alfred and her parents think you are one of God's gifts to that little girl

right now." He shifted toward her and Marlo caught his scent—
leather, horse and fresh air blended with a spicy aftershave.

"It was a mild heart condition that was her underlying problem.
The docs feel she can be treated and will live a normal life. She'll
have to be in the rehab hospital for physical therapy for some time,
but it could have been much worse. I talked to Alfred this
morning, and they've told him that they expect very good results."

"And how is Alfred? I haven't seen him out here much."

"He was a wreck, but as Cammi improves, he does, too. My
dad has been his rock through this." Jake scowled, which didn't
do a thing to harm his good looks. Marlo admired his chiseled
features and uncommonly long, dark eyelashes. "All this affected
my father, too. Out of the blue, he's telling me how important
children are and that I should have some of my own soon. He's
suddenly realized he's without heirs, other than me."

Compassion crept into his tone. "He met mortality face-to-
face. My father likes to be in control, and things aren't working
out his way. It's difficult for him."

Compassionate. Check. Jake was unvaryingly forgiving of
his father's idiosyncrasies. Marlo wished Jake didn't fit the List
so well. It would have been much easier to walk away from his
friendship.

"You're very different from him, aren't you?" The wind
whipped Marlo's short, dark hair into a frenzy. "You resemble
him physically, but not emotionally."

Jake automatically moved a strand of hair out of her eye. The
electricity that the innocent touch provoked startled her.

Dismayed, Marlo rubbed her arms to chase away goose
bumps that had nothing to do with the weather. Couldn't she even
stand next to the man without being affected by him? "Looks like
it will be an early fall," she said inanely.

"That reminds me, I freed up one of the indoor arenas for the therapy program. We're now capable of being open for business twelve months a year." He looked at her sharply. "What's wrong? Are those tears in your eyes?"

"Don't mind me, I'm being stupid." She scrubbed at her eye with the back of her hand. Suddenly, all the emotion she'd been so valiantly trying to subdue came to the surface.

Without a word, he took her by the arm and steered her toward a nearby stack of hay bales and set her down. His gaze worriedly scanned her face. "Marlo?"

"Sorry. I should be jumping for joy to hear that the program will run twelve months a year. I just feel like a bit of a failure myself right now."

He said nothing, but his body language told Marlo how intently he was listening.

"I've mentioned my nephew to you," she began softly, "but I haven't given you any details about him." She went on to tell Jake about the oxygen deprivation, of Brady's fearfulness and the resistance she met from Jenny every time she mentioned having Brady ride. "Having this open year-round will give me more time to get Jenny's permission to bring Brady here, but I don't hold out much hope. It's so frustrating to see children benefit from this and know that I can't even get the child closest to me to take part. My sister loves Brady so much that she doesn't realize that she's not letting him really *live.* I'm frozen by Jenny's resistance to suggestion where Brady is concerned."

"This is why this program means so much to you."

She nodded miserably. "But if I can't get Jenny to budge…."

"If your sister won't let him ride, at least have her and Brady come for a visit. Let her see that these horses aren't wild, firebreathing stallions."

She hesitated, not quite sure how to bring that about.

"You know, Marlo, it might change his life."

* * *

Marlo stood on her sister's front step and tried to build the courage to ring the bell. Three times she lifted her hand to press the buzzer, and three times she allowed her arm to drop to her side. Just as she was about to try again, the door flew open.

"What are you doing out here? Why didn't you walk in?" Jenny's blond hair was clipped at the nape of her neck, and she wore a hot-pink turtleneck sweater.

"I was building up courage."

"That's silly, you don't need courage to talk to me." Jenny led her to the kitchen. "Coffee, tea or chai?"

"Chai, please. Where's Brady?"

"He and his dad went to look for a storm door for the house. The way this weather is acting, it will be winter before we know it. I'll bet there's snow at Thanksgiving for Angela's wedding."

"She won't like that. It isn't in her plans."

"Even Angela can't arrange for good weather."

"If the television weather person gets threatening letters mid-November, we'll have a good idea who sent them." Marlo was glad for the cheerful banter. For what she was about to do, Jenny needed to be in a good mood.

"What is so scary that you had to talk yourself into ringing my doorbell? You aren't sick or anything? If there's something…"

Marlo held up her hand before Jenny could work herself into a lather. "I'm fine. No one is ill. In fact, I just got a letter from Aunt Tildy. She's taking riding lessons."

"Horse riding? At her age?"

"Motorcycles, actually…but now that you bring up the subject of horses, there is something I'd like to discuss with you."

Jenny's expression grew wary. "If it's about Brady going to Hammond Stables, forget it."

"Just come for a visit. It's taken on a life of its own, far beyond what Jake had envisioned. Now he's in discussion with a group who would like to have him start a therapeutic riding program, one in which the rider is in charge of the horse, not the therapist or horse expert. There's even preparation for the Special Olympics. Besides—" Marlo's voice turned pleading "—you've never been there to see what I'm doing. The My Own Pony program is a huge hit."

"What does Jake get out of this?" Jenny asked warily.

"Pleasure. Fun. Satisfaction. He has a disabled friend who's encouraged him to do this. I told him a little about Brady and he wants him to come."

"What is this, Marlo? Do you want Brady to be your 'cause'?" Jenny asked caustically.

"It's not like that, and you know it. I want you to see what is available for Brady, that's all."

"Everyone is ganging up on me." Jenny's voice shook with emotion. "Why can't you all leave me alone?"

"What do you mean, 'everyone'?"

"You, my husband, the doctor…you all want him to try all these things that are too dangerous! None of you understand!"

So she wasn't alone in her quest after all, Marlo thought. "At least come and see other kids ride. Brady doesn't need to do anything but watch. It might not be as dangerous as you imagine."

Jenny threw the dish towel she was holding on to the counter. "I vowed when Brady was tiny that I would never do anything foolish again. I was imprudent once and it's my fault he's the way he is, and…"

"It is not!" Marlo felt frustration rise within her like a geyser ready to blow. "No one blames you for anything. I don't get it, sis. When are you going to turn this over to God and allow Him to handle it?"

"I have."

"Then why don't you let Him help you?"

"I do… I have…."

"Forgive yourself and go on. God's willing to forgive and to forget." *As far as the east is from the west, so far He removes our transgression from us.*

"I've tried, Marlo. I've tried so many times. I'm not sure I know how."

"Then ask Him to show you how."

"Pray how to pray?" Jenny, her face red and blotchy, her eyes watering, looked so miserable that Marlo's heart ached for her.

She moved toward her sister and put an arm around her shoulders. "He'll show you. You'll know. I'm sure of it."

"Does it happen for you?"

"Yes, it does." Marlo thought of the sense she'd had all these weeks—God didn't want her chasing after Jake. He wanted her to wait on His direction. "I don't always know what He means, but I trust that someday I'll find it out."

Jenny's eyes cleared a little. "You're talking about Jake, aren't you? You love him. I can see it—and yet you do everything in your power to keep it platonic."

"I have to trust God's word, Jen, whether it makes sense or not."

"If you can walk out in trust, I guess I can, too."

Marlo's head snapped up, disbelief on her face.

"Brady and I will come out to Hammond Stables just to look around. He will not ride and you will not try to convince me that he should," Jenny said firmly. "We will visit, nothing more. That's my final offer."

"I accept. But if he really loves it…"

"Marlo, stop it."

"Okay, forget I said that." Marlo knew enough to quit while she was ahead. It was also time for her to go to work. "What day will you come?"

* * *

In the kitchen, Marlo hummed happily as she baked, knowing that Jenny had agreed to come to the stables. The Divas business had doubled, and more calls were coming in every day. Marlo had begun going in at 5:00 a.m. to begin food preparation. Lucy, meanwhile, was at her wits' end with arranging the catering end of things. Angela was a particular problem. According to Lucy, if any of them made it through the wedding without breaking down or cracking up it would be a wonder.

That afternoon Marlo headed for the stables. She was laying out curry combs and hoof picks for the My Own Pony children when a platinum-colored SUV drove slowly into the yard. Jake, who was sorting through halters for the kids to use, looked up. Marlo gazed at the car and glanced away before doing a double take.

"My sister Jenny is here!" Marlo clapped her hands to her cheeks. "She brought Brady!"

He caught up with her before she reached the car, took her by the elbow and turned her toward him. "Don't forget, Marlo, you've seen it yourself. Dreams can come true out here. Even for your nephew."

Optimistic. Check.

If she'd dared, she would have thrown her arms around him and kissed him hard. But that wasn't to be. Even if she didn't get her way, there was still hope for Brady.

Chapter Eighteen

"Auntie Marlo, pet the ponies?" Brady pulled at the leg of her jeans, his eyes shining brightly up at her.

"Oh, I don't think so, honey," Jenny interjected smoothly. "We're just here to *look* at the horses."

Marlo smiled weakly at the little boy. "I think I can find a pony just your size."

"Marlo!" Jenny said sharply. "You promised."

"No riding, but we didn't say anything about petting. Come on, Brady. Let's go over here." She took him to the area where a fat, shiny pony and two small, gentle-looking mares stood. "These are horses that live at Hammond Stables just to be petted, brushed and groomed," Marlo explained. "Mr. Hammond bought them so that the brothers and sisters of the children who come to ride can brush them."

"Bwush," Brady demanded.

"Brush," Jenny automatically corrected his pronunciation.

Marlo shot her a silencing look. She picked up a small curry comb and handed it to Brady. "Which pony do you want to comb?"

Without speaking, Brady headed for the fat black-and-white

pony. He showed none of the fear or trepidation Jenny had predicted he would. Under Marlo's supervision, he gently stroked the animal's round belly. When the pony turned its head to look at Brady the little boy looked back with wonder in his eyes.

Marlo turned to look at her sister. Tears were running down Jenny's cheeks and her shoulders were shaking with sobs.

Before Marlo could decide what her next move should be, she felt a warm presence beside her. Jake had returned. With his arm, he nudged her toward her sister. "Go to her. She's having a meltdown. I'll take care of Brady."

He turned to the child, who was now staring fearful and wide-eyed at his weeping mother. "Hey, buddy, let's brush the horse over here. Her name is Matilda. We call her Mattie for short. Can you say Mattie?" With little fuss, Brady was enticed to apply his curry comb to Mattie's hide. Soon he was giggling happily and listening to Jake spin stories about the marvelous creature Mattie was. The way Jake was praising the little horse, she might well have been able to leap tall buildings in a single bound and save every child in the universe from having to eat broccoli.

Jenny, in a very un-Jenny-like fashion, sat down on a nearby bench, looking morose. "What's going on, sis?" Marlo asked. "It's okay. Brady doesn't have to ride. Look how much fun he's having!"

Jake had picked up the small boy and was holding him so he could comb Mattie's forelock. The horse stood placidly, obviously enjoying the attention. Jake looked as natural with the child in his arms as Brady's own father might.

"I know. That's why I'm crying." Jenny hiccupped and blew her nose.

"What would you be doing if he was having a miserable time? Laughing?"

New tears welled in Jenny's eyes. "I'd be angry with you. I'd say, 'I told you so, I told you that this was no place for my son.' Don't you see? That's why I'm so upset!"

Marlo didn't, but she held her tongue, waiting for Jenny to go on.

"I've always tried to do what I thought was best for Brady, to keep him out of situations I thought would be frightening or dangerous—like allowing him around horses." Jenny's eyes fixed on her smiling son. Brady had thrown one arm around Jake's neck and was patting Mattie's neck with his free hand. "Now look at him. I haven't seen him smile like that in forever. All my protecting him, making sure the kids in my day care didn't play rough around him, not letting him run because he might fall…" Jenny looked up at Marlo with a piteous expression.

Marlo had told her sister this a hundred times and in a hundred ways, but Jenny had always been impervious to suggestion and unyielding in her opinions about how her son should be raised. For the past five years no one, sometimes not even Jenny's own husband, could make her see that Brady was tougher than she gave him credit for—a real little boy, not a porcelain facsimile.

"I've made a mess of things again, haven't I?" Jenny said.

Something snapped inside Marlo. "Jenny, quit being so selfish! Get over yourself."

Jenny gasped audibly. "What do you mean? I'd give my life for Brady!"

"You have already. But you've taken Brady's life away in the process."

Brady was now smattering kisses on Mattie's forehead. Marlo had never seen him so animated. "Quit hanging on to the idea that any of this is your fault. Quit protecting him! Look at the wonderful things he is able to accomplish. I see children like Brady blossom every day. Get over it, Jenny. Allow Brady to have a life."

Marlo hadn't realized it, but she, too, had begun to cry. All the love, concern, apprehension and tenderness she felt for her sister and her nephew swirled within her in a dizzying kaleidoscope of emotion.

"I don't think I know how." The soft words slipped through Jenny's lips. "I'm not you, Marlo. I'm not brave and funny and daring. I'm cautious, timid and fearful—even more so after Brady was born." She held her hands in tight fists, skin taut, knuckles white. "I don't know how to let go."

Silently Marlo took her sister's hand in her own. One by one, she pried Jenny's fingers open until her open palm lay flat against Marlo's hand. "Like this.

"Every time you experience anxiety, open your palms and offer what you are holding to God. Imagine whatever it is you're grappling with floating away. He's waiting to catch it, Jenny."

"How can I 'let go,' when Brady is an ever-present reminder?"

"Give it to God again—and again—and again. He'll help you break the habit of guilt and of fear."

"Since when are guilt and fear a 'habit'?"

"What's that Chinese proverb? 'You cannot prevent the birds of worry and care from flying over your head, but you can stop them from building a nest in your hair.' You may feel guilty or fearful, but you don't have to allow that to inhabit your whole life." Marlo squeezed her sister's upturned hands. "Be brave for Brady, even if you can't be for yourself."

Jenny, tears still streaming down her face, gave a weak smile. "And you have a suggestion for the first thing I should be brave about, don't you? You want me to let Brady ride."

"You said Brady's doctor thought it was okay. Ask him again. If he wants Brady to do it, then you can be brave."

"Mommy cwying?" Brady, still in Jake's arms, leaned out toward his mother as Jake carried him to Jenny.

"It's okay, honey. I think these tears are turning into a happy cry." She scooped him out of Jake's arms. "Sorry, I didn't mean to get you involved in anything emotional. As you can tell, Marlo is persistent when she puts her mind to something...fortunately."

"If it is any comfort, I'll do everything in my power to keep Brady safe if he does come here to ride," Jake said gently. "I'll handle the horse myself. I know every one of these animals like they were family. Marlo has turned into an excellent side-walker, too. I'm not sure Brady could fall off the horse even if he wanted to."

"Then there is no time like the present," Marlo agreed.

Jenny stared at her, aghast.

"She's right, you know," Jake said. "I have time. Let's do it." He took Jenny's hand. "It will be fine. Really."

Jenny was speechless, but when she didn't protest, Jake took that as an assent.

As Jake saddled Mattie he talked to Brady, explaining each and every thing he was doing and what each piece of equipment was for. Jake even explained the use for Brady's helmet, and how he, Marlo and Mattie would be taking care of the child every instant. "Some horses give a lot of lateral movement, while others give more rotation," he told Jenny. "I think Mattie will be a good choice for Brady."

Jenny seemed to be as comforted by Jake's calm, soothing patter as was her son. When Jake lifted Brady into the saddle, however, Jenny looked away.

Brady, unlike his mother, showed no fear whatsoever. Instead, he giggled happily and commanded, "Go, Mattie!"

"Let's get a little more help first, buddy. We need side-walkers for both sides of the horse. Marlo, you lead Mattie and I'll be on the watch for Brady."

Jenny stepped up, silently took Jake's instruction and stepped close to the horse's side.

Marlo moved out, leading Mattie at a snail's pace. Brady's body swayed a bit at first, but he soon caught on to the rhythmic gait and settled in for the ride. As they walked slowly around the round pen Brady squealed happily. The docile Mattie never even twitched an ear. "Look, Mommy, I'm fwying!"

"Yes, honey, you're flying." Jenny mopped at her eyes and blew her nose.

Two, three, four times around the ring they went. Jake and the horse were as patient as Job, Marlo observed. They'd be willing to do this for hours if it was what Brady wanted—and he probably did. It was Jenny she was worried about. Jenny was alternately crying and laughing until she had to be ready for an emotional washout.

"I think this is enough for today, honey," she told Brady.

"I want to wide."

"Then we'll make an appointment for another day, okay? We don't want Mattie to wear out, do we?"

The idea that the horse might be tired was motivation enough for compassionate Brady. Already bonded to this animal, he didn't want to do anything to harm it. Jake tied Mattie and held out his arms to Brady, who slid happily into them. The child threw himself around Jake and gave him a big, noisy kiss on the cheek.

"You've been adopted into the family," Marlo told Jake. "Brady only hugs and kisses very special people."

"I'm honored." Jake's expression was one of delight. "This is exactly what I imagined happening when I decided to start the program. Here it is, my dream come true."

Marlo walked her sister and Brady back to the car. Jenny touched Marlo's cheek with the tip of her finger and, words escaping her, slid silently into the driver's seat. As they drove off, Brady looked back to smile and wave, not at Marlo, but at the horse.

When they'd gone, Marlo turned to Jake. "I think this calls for a celebration."

A slow smile spread over Jake's features. "What did you have in mind?"

"I'm having a party this weekend." She steeled herself to add, "Bring Sabrina."

Jake looked taken aback. "I…ah…well, sure. We'd love to. At least *I* would. I'll check with Sabrina. Thank you. Just tell me where and when."

"My place, Saturday night. Come about seven. The dress is summer wear. Shorts, sleeveless tops, flip-flops, muscle shirts, bathing suits if you dare. We'll be having appetizers first and dinner later. Steaks or ribs, so come hungry."

"Shorts and flip-flops? Have you noticed the temperature lately, Marlo? Or the chill in the air? By the look of it, we have an early—and cold—fall."

"I didn't ask you to critique either the weather or the dress code," she said cheerfully. "Are you coming or not?"

"I'll be there for sure. We'll see about Sabrina."

Chapter Nineteen

Had Jake convinced Sabrina to attend the party? Marlo wondered, as she wheeled a child's wagon full of sand through the patio door and dumped it into a child's plastic swimming pool on her living-room floor. Marlo propped a striped beach umbrella in the sand and tossed a brightly colored sand bucket and plastic shovel into the mix. Sabrina would probably arrive in a sequin-spangled sarong and Jimmy Choo sandals—if, that is, she believed Jake when he told her about the dress code for the party.

Lucy rolled a wheelbarrow filled with sand through the patio door and Marlo pointed to the other plastic pools in the room which could use a little more sand. Then she eyeballed the patio lights and paper lanterns strung around the room and on the deck outside. "Dad is practically salivating. He wants to come to this party so badly," Lucy commented. "He's heard about your summer parties for years."

Lucy had borrowed her father's old record player and every LP or single that had the words *summer, beach* or *love* in the title. She'd also found dozens of kooky beach movies from the sixties and a VHS player to play them on, which she'd managed to set up on continuous play in the basement.

"Invite him. He can be our DJ, as long as he promises not to do his Elvis impersonations. After all, I invited Jake and Sabrina."

"You did *what?* You invited I'm-too-good-for-the-likes-of-you Sabrina to your home?"

"She's part of Jake's life." It was one of the most difficult things she'd ever done, extending that invitation, but she knew it was the right thing to do. She refused to be cast in the role of the "other woman," no matter how much she cared about Jake.

"Does Jake talk about marrying Sabrina?" Lucy asked.

"Everyone does it for him, his father especially, and Sabrina."

"He doesn't seem like the kind of guy who'd be railroaded into anything."

Marlo caught a glimpse of herself in the mirror she'd decorated with sea shells and starfish. Her short, dark hair stood on end, her cheeks were ruddy from exertion and her eyes were wide. She could be the poster child for wholesomeness, innocence and possibly naïveté.

Jake wasn't being railroaded, she mused. Sabrina was perfection. Why would he be interested in her, a long-legged Kewpie doll, when Sabrina was available?

What's more, a verse from I John 2 had been popping into her mind a lot lately: *By this we may be sure that we know Him, if we obey His commandment. Whoever says, "I abide in him," ought to walk as He walked.* That was all she was trying to do, walk as Jesus walked and do what He would think was right. It wasn't easy, but maybe God had plans for her that she couldn't see until the time was right. It was like the passage in Corinthians about seeing through a glass darkly. Right now she was viewing her future through deeply tinted glass, but someday God would show her clearly what she was to do.

Satisfied that her kitchen was in order, Marlo went into the bedroom and put on a sleeveless sundress and a pair of strappy heels that made her legs appear to go on forever. Glad that the sunless tanning lotion had done its job, she put on an ankle bracelet and a Hawaiian lei made of silk flowers.

When she was about to leave the room, she stopped to check her makeup in the dresser mirror. Stuck into one corner between the mirror and its frame was the piece of paper Jenny had given her the day of the Bridesmaids' Luncheon. Next to it was a silly photo of her and Jake that Cammi had snapped with a disposable camera and given to her. Slowly Marlo reached for the note, the Cinderella List.

"Thoughtful, courteous, compassionate, faithful to God, hospitable, intuitive…" Those were the qualities of her Prince Charming that stood out now. Her perfect prince existed on the *inside* of a man, not the outside. Handsome didn't matter; neither did wealth, or fame or prestige. Ironically, she'd found a prince who had it all when she met Jake. And the prince would never be hers.

She folded the paper and took down the photo of her and Jake mugging for the camera and put them both in the bottom drawer, out of sight, but not yet out of mind.

Marlo went to the patio door to check the outside thermometer. Thirty-eight degrees. A damp, gusty wind made the trees in the yard slant in one direction. All in all, a miserable night—cold, wet and windy. Perfect.

She turned up the thermostat to a balmy eighty-five degrees and straightened the wall hanging that proclaimed, "Be fishers of men. If you'll catch them, He'll clean them," before answering the doorbell. Bridesmaid Club members Linda, Becky and Christine and their spouses hustled into the room in various kinds of beach attire under their thick jackets. Jenny and her husband arrived in his and hers grass skirts and colorful but ridiculous-looking sun hats.

"Angela called just as we were leaving. She's come down with a terrible cold and she sends her regrets," Jenny told Marlo. "I guess we'll have to hear about the matrimonial extravaganza another day." Marlo was too gracious to say she was relieved. Angela had been haunting the Divas kitchen for days, and even a caterer could talk about a wedding only so much.

After that, the stream of guests was steady until only Jake and Sabrina were missing. Lucy's father fired up the music and a loud, off-key sing-along erupted.

"Do you think I should start grilling steaks and putting out the ribs?" Lucy wore a bikini over silk long johns. "I saw someone try to take a bite out of the mango hanging on the fake palm tree."

This particular party had become an instant tradition five years ago, when, in the dead of winter, Marlo had decided to take advantage of her skewed sense of humor and reputation for doing things backward and have a beach party on the coldest day in February. This year she'd moved up the date, since the early cold snap had made all her friends grumpy. There was nothing like a party to cheer people up.

People, that was, other than poor, lovesick Bryan, who had come, but announced that he wasn't staying long. Lonesome and not in a party mood, he sat under a beach umbrella in one of the kiddy pools, talking to her cousin Kelly on his cell.

"I guess Jake and Sabrina aren't coming," Marlo admitted ruefully. "You might as well heat the grills."

Bobbing her head, Lucy trudged toward the patio. Marlo made a turn around the room to make sure everyone was enjoying a moment of summer on this miserable, wintry night. As she passed the thermostat, she bumped the temperature up to ninety.

She was near the front door when the doorbell rang. Marlo threw open the door and Jake and Sabrina entered on a gust of wind and cold, pelting rain.

"Welcome to the beach party! Take off your coats, kick off your shoes and walk in the sand," she greeted them. "Lucy's firing up the grill and we'll be eating soon."

The looks on Jake's and Sabrina's faces were worth the entire effort of the party, Marlo decided. Dumbstruck, they stared into the room before them. In one of the kiddy pools, someone had dumped water in order to have a miniature sand castle–building contest. The spouses of the Bridesmaid Club were lip-synching to old tunes. Even though the party guests were in shorts and T-shirts, the room was hot enough to cause sweat to pour down their faces. Others had sprawled out in the beach chairs Marlo had provided, and were tanning under the fake orange sun she'd lit from behind with a floodlight from her garage. Everyone, it appeared, was having a wonderful time.

"I guess you were telling me the truth when you said 'dress for summer,'" Jake said.

"I never lie," Marlo said cheerfully. "May I take your coats?"

Sabrina stood frozen, as a deer in headlights.

Jake helped her with her jacket. Beneath it was a strapless party dress. "I told her to dress for summer and she didn't believe me. This was the best she would do."

"You were actually serious?" Sabrina found her voice. "What *is* this?"

"My annual beach party. A taste of summer when we need it most. Would you like a fruit kabob?"

"Who on earth would think of this except you?" Jake appeared as amused as Sabrina was dumbstruck.

"Join the fun. There's a game of plastic horseshoes going on in the basement, and someone was trying to find something to use as a net and a ball for minivolleyball. The only rules are to have fun, eat plenty and try to break as few things as possible."

Before he could say more, Marlo excused herself to refill the punch bowl. She couldn't allow herself to dwell on any part of the situation with Jake and Sabrina. Besides, they'd been to plenty of parties. They should surely be able to navigate this one.

By midnight, many had made their exit, but those who remained made no signs of departing. The kitchen counter looked like a graveyard, covered in rib and steak bones. All the food was gone except for a bowl of tapioca pudding, which Marlo loved and everyone she knew hated. It was her way of ensuring that there would be leftovers in the morning.

Jake had moved easily in the crowd, introducing himself to everyone. Sabrina had stayed glued to his side, meeting people graciously, but continuing to look as if she'd been hit with a stun gun.

All the while, Marlo deftly managed to be where Jake was not, even though she was always perfectly aware of his whereabouts in the room. Finally, she put on a pair of orange sunglasses so that no one would see her gazing longingly at him.

As midnight neared, the frozen expression on Sabrina's features relaxed somewhat. The woman was out of her element, but she was still game. Marlo gave Sabrina big points for not throwing a tantrum and insisting that Jake take her home immediately.

In fact, at the moment, Sabrina sat forlornly on the couch, with Jake nowhere in sight. The yelling coming from the basement, where the foosball table was located, hinted at where he might be.

Marlo edged in her direction. "Can I get you anything?" She lowered her voice. "I've got another key lime pie stashed away."

"I'm fine, thanks." Sabrina's hands fluttered nervously. "The food was wonderful. You are an amazing cook."

Marlo sat down on a chair across from Sabrina. "Well, considering what I do for a living, I'm glad to hear it."

"I…I've never been to a party quite like this one."

"No? I suppose not. I've done this for so long that a beach party when the temperature dips makes perfect sense to me." Marlo liked this softer, more unsure Sabrina. "How's Cammi? I didn't stop by today because I've been preparing for the party."

Sabrina's expression brightened. "She's told me how much she appreciates your visits."

"How is Alfred?"

"Nervous. He'd move mountains to help Cammi, if he could." Sabrina studied Marlo. "He likes you, you know."

Marlo felt a softening in her chest. For the first time, she could say the same about Sabrina. "Hey, are you sure you don't want any key lime pie?"

It was fascinating to see Sabrina relax and unwind as they sat at Marlo's kitchen table. She was funny and charming and Marlo could see why Jake enjoyed spending time with her.

Jake found the two of them in the kitchen, eating directly out of the pie pan with soup spoons, and laughing as Marlo regaled Sabrina with stories about previous beach parties. His eyes widened as he took in the sight. "Do you have another fork, ladies?"

"In the drawer by the sink. There's also tapioca pudding in the refrigerator, in case you'd rather have that," Marlo offered idly. No one ever ate the tapioca.

"Tapioca? I haven't had that in years. It used to be my favorite dessert." Jake took a spoon from the drawer.

Wouldn't you know it? Marlo thought, as she watched Jake dish up a bowl of pudding. He was the one man she'd ever met who was enthusiastic about white goop with a rubbery texture, and he already belonged to someone else.

"Thanks for everything." Jake and Sabrina put their jackets

on over their summer clothing as they prepared to leave. "It was...memorable."

Marlo kept a smile cemented to her face until they'd disappeared into Jake's car. Only then could she allow her true feelings to show.

Chapter Twenty

"She was nicer than I expected her to be," Lucy said the next morning, as they cleared up the detritus left from the party. "Sabrina, I mean."

"Maybe we've only seen her at her worst," Marlo said, as she filled a recycling bin with plastic soda bottles. "She was softer last night, more real."

"She didn't leave Jake's side for most of the evening."

"I wouldn't either, if he were my boyfriend."

Lucy sat down and put her elbows on the counter. "It hurts, doesn't it? Are you going to tell him how you feel?"

"Call me crazy, but I won't risk breaking up a relationship." The way Marlo saw it, if God wanted Jake and her together, He would make it happen. And if He didn't want it, she didn't either, no matter how much it hurt right now.

"You're too good for your own good," Lucy muttered, as she piled flatware and glasses into the dishwasher. "No, I take that back. I'm in awe. You're stronger than any other woman I know."

"Once she let her hair down, Sabrina was actually fun." Marlo scrubbed at a pan. "I can see why she and Jake are comfortable together. They know each other so well. I suppose that happens when you practically grow up together."

"You are much more charitable than I would be."

Charitable? She wasn't charitable, only obedient... *We love the children of God, when we love God and obey His commandments.*

Marlo felt compelled to be gracious to Sabrina, and the nicer she was, the easier it had become. Another one of God's lessons. Love begets love. What God hadn't done was offer Jake to her on a silver platter. Instead, what He'd asked of her was to wait for His timing. All she could do was wait for whatever He had planned next.

Her afternoon free, Marlo decided it was a good time to visit Cammi at the rehabilitation wing of the hospital.

Marlo took the elevator to the third floor, but it was not Cammi she found in the room. Sabrina sat in a vinyl recliner, staring vacantly out the window at the parking lot.

At least it looked a little like Sabrina. The makeup-free blonde woman with her hair pulled back in a ponytail, wearing tattered jeans and a lime-green blouse, was hunched forward with a vacant expression on her face.

"Sabrina?" Marlo ventured, stepping into the room. "Where's Cammi?"

Sabrina jumped, startled, as if her thoughts had been far away. "She's in the swimming pool. The therapist says she's really responding to it. They may let her go home tomorrow, and do therapy on an outpatient basis."

A good-looking young man who'd been sitting in a chair in the far corner jumped to his feet. He had light brown hair, stylishly cut, and a kind face. "I think I'll go downstairs and pick up a paper, Brina. I'll be back. Do you want anything?"

"No, thanks, Randy," Sabrina said absently. Marlo noticed how surprisingly young and vulnerable she looked.

"I've been really scared for her." Sabrina touched her finger to her cheek. "So scared I get up in the morning and come here without even putting makeup on. I must look a mess."

"You look beautiful," Marlo said, and meant it.

"You're always so nice." Sabrina's lips softened into a smile. "Sometimes I wonder why."

Marlo pulled up a chair across from her. "What do you mean by that?"

"I haven't exactly greeted you with open arms, but you've never been less than polite and friendly." Sabrina tucked her feet onto the seat of the chair and wrapped her arms around her knees. "I couldn't have done that. I even asked Jake about it."

Marlo felt a nervous trill run through her. "What did he say?"

"Something about your policy of 'turning the other cheek.' He said it was in the Bible."

"I see."

"Jake is a Christian man," Sabrina informed Marlo. "He doesn't talk about it much, at least not around his father, who thinks faith is just another name for hocus-pocus, but it's important to him. He says you're a Christian, too. That's why he understands you so well."

"Do you and Jake talk about a lot of things like that?"

Sabrina smiled, amused. "I've known Jake all my life. It's difficult to not cover a lot of territory in that time."

"You care for him a great deal, don't you?" Marlo couldn't help but say it. It was so obvious to her from the way Sabrina said Jake's name and the look she had in her eyes when she talked about him.

"I love him with all my heart. You've threatened me since day one," Sabrina added candidly, surprising Marlo with her honesty. "Randall and Alfred have always talked about how wonderful it would be if the Randalls and the Dorchesters could be one big, happy family. For that to happen, Jake and I would have to marry." She looked appraisingly at Marlo. "But I see how much he likes you. He thinks you are funny, sweet and beautiful." She tugged thoughtfully at the casual ponytail she wore. "He's always preferred brunettes like you to blondes like me. But the one time I decided to darken my hair, he hated it on me."

"I don't know what to say," Marlo admitted.

"You don't have to say anything. I just felt like telling you, that's all. Cammi's accident has shown me that life is short. I can't wait around for things that might not happen, and there's no point being anything but honest."

"I'd never get between you and Jake if you were planning to marry. Never. I can promise you that."

"How can you be so sure?" Sabrina's eyes narrowed and suspicion flooded her expression.

"I was engaged to a man I loved with all my heart. Before we married, I discovered that he was seeing someone else. I promised myself then and there that I would not do to another woman what was done to me. It's as simple as that. You have nothing to fear from me."

"I'm not sure it matters anymore." Sabrina unfolded her knees and stretched.

"What do you mean?"

"Even if you never come between us physically, Jake has changed since he met you. A lot."

"I'll quit volunteering at the stables," Marlo said, her determination underscored by this bit of information. "He'll forget about me quickly enough."

"See?" Sabrina said, waving a finger in Marlo's face. "That's why I like you, even if I don't want to. You are generous to a fault." She smiled faintly. "And your generosity brings out my flaws."

"I'm not the family choice for Jake," Marlo said wryly. "You are. Randall barely tolerates me. I know he thinks I'm treading on your territory."

"There you go again, making me like you when I don't want to," Sabrina said almost morosely.

Marlo had to smile. She understood perfectly. The feeling was mutual.

Before either of them could say more, Cammi returned to the room in a wheelchair pushed by her therapist, and her face lit with pleasure at the sight of two of her favorite people.

Only two days later, the sight that met Marlo as she drove into the farmyard made her gasp with delight. Cammi, dressed in a riding habit, was with her grandfather and gazing up at one of the therapy horses.

"I want to ride Feather, Grandpa," Cammi was saying, when Marlo neared. "I don't know this horse."

"This is therapy, Cammi. Feather will have to wait until you are stronger. I don't want you to take a tumble."

"Feather wouldn't let that happen. She practically saved me when I got sick. You told me so. She stood perfectly still for me." Cammi thrust her lower lip out to make a little pink shelf. Then she saw Marlo and the pout disappeared. "Marlo!"

"Hi, honey." Marlo hugged her. "I'm so glad I'm here to see your first ride."

"It's baby stuff," Cammi said disdainfully.

"Give it a try anyway. Humor us."

Cammi turned at the sound of Jake's voice. A beautiful smile broke across her features. "Uncle Jake!"

He gathered Cammi in his arms and the three of them were laughing together about the ribbon Cammi wanted woven into Feather's tail.

This was an answered prayer.

Chapter Twenty-One

Lucy was lying on the couch in the Divas' small, carpeted office when Marlo arrived at work.

"Didn't you go home last night?" Marlo offered a hand and pulled her friend to her feet.

"I meant to. At ten o'clock, when I was about to leave, Angela called. Now she's considering pork tenderloin with stuffing, and cheesy potatoes, plus vegetarian lasagna for the vegans. She's also asked for a coffee bar, so that people can have exactly what they want at the reception. I told her caffeinated and decaf were enough, but, no, she says we should offer mochas, lattes, cappuccinos and a variety of teas. Now we've got to find a barista to deal with that."

Lucy eyed Marlo speculatively. "And she wants to know the name of your date, for the place cards. The calligrapher is getting anxious about not having all the names."

"Lucy, when you marry, promise that you won't do this to me?"

"Are you kidding? My idea of wedding food is hot dogs on the grill and a sundae bar with endless ice cream." She yawned widely and stretched her arms over her head. "Angela says she's been trying to call you for days to find out who your date will be. Will you please turn your cell phone back on?"

"That's the very reason I don't have my cell phone on—I don't have a date. Everyone I know is married." She'd considered everyone, from the postman to the cute guy that delivered the produce. Then she'd tried to think of someone she knew from church or the gym, all to no avail.

Marlo sank onto a stool. "Maybe I'll have to hire someone to take me," she said gloomily.

"Why don't you just ask Jake?"

"It's not a good idea, Lucy. I'm playing with fire when I'm around him. I like him too much, and he belongs to Sabrina."

"You have volunteered untold hours for his project at Hammond Stables. The way I see it, he *owes* you something."

"I didn't do it for payback, Lucy." But she was desperate, and it was tempting. Maybe she could consider asking Jake to escort her, if she viewed it like her time at the stables—a gift she wanted to give, a positive contribution to another's life.

She saw a bowl of rising bread dough Lucy had started sometime before dawn sitting on the counter. Marlo punched her entire fist into the bowl and with great satisfaction watched the air leak out and the dough sink to the bottom of the dish. How had she gotten herself into such a mess?

After a day of preparation for Angela's wedding, Marlo went home early. She hadn't been in the house more than a few minutes when an unanticipated surprise arrived on her doorstep. A tall woman with short-cropped hair, in a pair of stylish jeans, an oversize white shirt and enough turquoise jewelry to anchor a rowboat, opened her arms and squealed at the sight of Marlo.

"Aunt Tildy! What are you doing here?"

The exotic-looking woman matched Marlo's height inch for inch, and she was thin as a willow. She dropped her suitcase on the porch and flung her arms around her niece, enveloping her in a haze of Chanel No. 5, Tildy's signature scent. "You're more beautiful than ever!"

"I look just like you, remember?" Marlo's voice was muffled, buried as she was in her aunt's shoulder.

"Then you are exquisite, darling." Tildy released her. "Are you going to ask me in?" She sailed through the door, leaving her suitcase outside.

Laughing, Marlo picked it up and followed her aunt into the house. "This is an unexpected surprise. I thought you were off on a photo shoot in Africa or having sno-cones at the North Pole."

"Don't I wish! But I've done the next best thing and come here."

"What if I hadn't been home?" Tildy's unfortunate impulsiveness had been one of her genetic gifts to Marlo.

"You're always at home, darling, or at the kitchen. You work so hard that I knew you'd never go too far afield. Besides, I wanted to visit my lawn ornaments. They look very nice in your yard." Tildy moved through the house like a fresh breeze, touching trinkets she'd given Marlo over the years. "And if you weren't home, I'd go to Jenny's. That dear girl is practically afraid to leave house. How's sweet little Brady these days?"

"He's a love, as usual. Can I get you something? Tea? I've got a coffee cake."

When they were seated at Marlo's kitchen table, Tildy leaned her elbows on the table and stared into Marlo's eyes, ones much like her own. "Now tell me what's wrong."

"Who said anything was wrong?" Marlo filled two mugs with a Colombian brew.

"I have known you since the day of your birth. You stayed with me for weeks every summer. And much to your parents' dismay, we have similar personalities. You're sad. It's written all over your face."

Marlo might be able to keep something from Jenny or Jake, but with Tildy, it was useless. She might as well spill it all now, because her aunt would pry it out of her anyway. "I'm exhausted. My partner, Lucy, and I are catering a very big wedding next weekend. The bride is a friend of ours and she's very particular. I'm afraid Lucy might murder her before the wedding starts if she changes the menu one more time."

"And…" Tildy beckoned her to continue.

"I'm one of Angela's bridesmaids, and I have no idea how I can be in two places at once. Plus, the bride *insists* I bring a date, and I've run out of single men to invite."

"So your business is booming, you don't have enough help, you're in that always-a-bridesmaid, never-a-bride mood and there is no man in you life. No wonder you're blue! I arrived just in time to help you through this."

Marlo doubted that even Tildy could sort out the mess her life was becoming.

They began their two-woman slumber party even before nightfall. Tildy wore her shimmering, salmon-colored silk pajamas and slip-on mules with feathers. Marlo, not even attempting to match her aunt's glamour, put on a pair of oversize boxer shorts and a Minnesota Gophers sweatshirt. On the coffee table, she'd placed still-warm caramel corn with peanuts, a jug of iced tea, soft pretzels with honey mustard, beef jerky sticks and a coconut cake she'd had in the freezer.

"I'm glad I inherited your metabolism," Marlo said offhandedly, as she spooned mustard over a pretzel. "More cake?"

"Later, darling, I must get to the bottom of things before I eat another bite."

"There is no bottom to get to, Tildy. Trust me. Things are very clear-cut in my life right now."

"That's always been the problem with you, Marlo. Sometimes you seem blind to shades of gray. Everything is always black and white as far as you're concerned."

"This certainly is." Marlo sighed, put her feet on the puffy footstool and prepared herself to tell Tildy the long, sometimes painful story of her and Jake. When she was done—down to the smallest detail, and including the Cinderella List, her predicament about a date for the wedding and Lucy's suggestion that she invite Jake—she cut herself a piece of cake the size she usually called "dessert for two" and began to eat.

"That's it?" Tildy asked.

"Isn't that enough?" Even coconut cake wasn't doing it for Marlo tonight. She wondered if there was any mocha ice cream left in the freezer.

"I think Lucy is right. You *should* ask Jake to accompany you to the wedding. Treat it as purely business, a payback for the hours you've given him. If there's nothing between you—or you want to signal that there isn't—what better way to show him but with a formal business request? Darling, you told me you needed a place-filler, not a Prince Charming, for the wedding. Why *not* ask Jake?"

Why not? Marlo thought, resigned. According to the List, Jake was her Prince Charming, even though she'd make sure he never knew it. She would invite him just like Lucy and Tilly wanted her to, even though the idea of being with Jake when he wasn't hers was a little like picking her heart apart one piece at a time.

Chapter Twenty-Two

"You're a great sport, Tildy, to hang around and lend a hand to get us through this wedding." Marlo sank onto a stool in the Divas' kitchen for a quick respite from slicing vegetables for the lasagna.

Tildy, her sleeves rolled to her elbows, was patiently working on the handmade mints. "Not a problem, but you are still going to need more help than I can give you."

"I've been trying to come up with a solution—who does a caterer hire when she needs catering? It seems a little redundant."

"You don't need temporary help, Marlo. You need someone permanent, a partner in the business. I've seen your calendar. You and Lucy will wear yourselves out if you don't make changes."

"I agree. But who…" An idea came to her, but it would never work unless she made the offer tantalizing enough. Marlo dusted her hands on her apron. "If you'll excuse me, Aunt Tildy, I have an errand to run. Maybe I do have a solution for this problem after all."

When she returned later, Tildy and Lucy were sipping tea in the back room. "I leave and you two quit working? Is that how it is?"

"Our feet were killing us," Lucy said plaintively. "Besides, we're talking about you asking Jake to the wedding."

"Great. Date by committee. This whole thing is giving me a headache." She made tea for herself and started to move a stack of recipe books off a chair, so that she could sit down.

"Sometimes a committee can be a good thing," Lucy said smugly.

Marlo never trusted her friend when she had that tone in her voice. It always meant she was up to something. "What does that mean?"

"It means that Jake called with some questions about a fundraiser he's considering for the hippotherapy program. I told him that he should come in and talk to you."

Come in? "But you said you'd take over the Hammond account, remember. I don't need to get involved." At that moment the doorbell rang at the front of the shop.

"It's the perfect time for you to ask him to the wedding. Don't keep him waiting."

Marlo slunk to the front, dragging her low self-esteem behind her. How humiliating…and unfortunately, since the wedding was nearly upon her, how necessary.

Jake was studying a book of wedding cake photos and appeared particularly interested in one with a bride and groom trotting around the outer rim of the cake in an old-fashioned horse and buggy. He looked up when she entered, and a smile broke across his features.

He was more handsome than any other man she'd ever seen, Marlo thought. *Why me? Why now?*

"You appear to have the weight of the world on your shoulders." His expression softened into concern.

"It's because I have something very embarrassing to ask you." One of his eyebrows arched slightly.

"It's a business proposition, actually." Marlo's voice quavered a bit, and she steeled herself. "I never meant that volunteering at Hammond Stables should require any payback, but I need a favor and I've run out of options. I thought you might help me…just for a few hours…." Her voice trailed away. "It's a business favor, really." She scowled. "I'm sorry. I'm doing this very badly."

He smiled, seeming to enjoy her discomfiture. "Why don't you just spit it out? You've been a lifesaver at the stables. I probably owe you hundreds of hours. What is it you want me to do?"

"I…ah… The Divas are catering a wedding this weekend. The bride is a friend of Lucy's and mine, and she insists that if we don't bring dates we'll throw off her table settings. It's not convenient to have a date, because we'll be in the kitchen most of the evening, so it won't be much fun for whoever escorts me." She took a deep breath and sighed. "And I don't have anyone else I can ask." There. It was out. Pathetic 101.

Jake looked mildly confused. "Don't have anyone? What about your boyfriend, Bryan?"

Things were going from bad to worse, Marlo decided, but she might as well get it all out on the table at once. "Bryan's not exactly my boyfriend. He's a dear friend, but he's in love with my cousin. I'm just 'man-sitting' him for her while she's in boot camp in the army. Bryan's very lonesome, and Kelly thought it would be good for him to hang out with me. We've known each other forever."

His lip was quivering with either a laugh or a frown. "I'd be honored to escort you to your friend's wedding," he said formally, "on a purely business level."

Relief seeped through her body. "Thank you. You have no idea how silly I feel about this."

"No worries, just give me the time and address, and I'll be there. By the way," Jake continued, "do you let everyone call you 'pookie'?" Marlo flushed crimson from head to toe.

"That was embarrassing," Marlo said, when she returned to the kitchen after Jake had left with his fundraiser questions answered. "I hope I'm not going to hurt Sabrina by doing this. It is purely business."

"We know that and God knows that," Aunt Tildy said. "Let Him handle it. You are obviously willing to do whatever He requires of you, and you certainly keep getting thrown in with this man. Maybe it's coincidence and maybe not. Time will tell."

"I'm surprised at you, Tildy."

"Everyone always is." Her aunt smiled serenely.

It wasn't going to be an issue, having Jake as an escort, Marlo decided on the day of Angela's wedding. She'd been at the reception hall since 6:00 a.m., and Jake would drive here alone, sit in the seat next to hers and go home alone. She doubted she'd even have much time to talk to him. It couldn't get much more businesslike than that. Despite Angela's difficult and demanding ways, particularly about the escort issue, Marlo gave her credit for one thing—the bridesmaid dress. Finally, one of her friends had gotten it right. Angela had chosen black, a trend Marlo thought a bit funereal, but liked anyway. The dress was a simple sheath that skimmed her figure and accented her height and slenderness. She was happy to have a dress that was a real keeper.

An hour before the wedding was to begin, Marlo, Lucy and the individual who Marlo had begun referring to as "the solution to all our catering problems," were checking details and discussing timing. None of them even heard Jake until he cleared his throat to announce his presence.

He was in a classically cut, dark navy suit, and wore it with a white shirt and silk tie that reminded her of an impressionist painting. He nearly took her breath away. She opened her mouth to speak, but realized that Jake wasn't even looking at her. He was looking past her to the short man in a tall white hat.

"Franco?" he said, sounding stunned. "What are you doing here? Aren't you supposed to be at your restaurant?"

Franco, in a pleated chef's hat and apron as white as Jake's shirt, beamed. "Your friend Marlo hired me to work here tonight." He gestured toward the meticulously laid-out kitchen. "I am enjoying it immensely. It reminds me of my days on the cruise ship."

"You are full of surprises, aren't you?" Jake said to Marlo.

"Franco is a genius. I knew that from the first moment I tasted his food. Lucy and I have decided to work smarter, not harder, and Franco was the first person who came to mind. In fact, we're already discussing a way of bringing Franco in as a partner in Dining with Divas. We could easily double our business with his help. And possibly get a day off," Marlo added, suppressing a yawn. "We've been working twelve-hour days all week."

"Is that the reason I haven't seen you at the stables much lately?" Jake asked softly.

"Partly. I…."

Franco walked up to them with a dish towel in hand to shoo her off. "It's time for you to dress for the wedding, Marlo. Lucy, too. I'll take over now."

"We can't leave yet—it's too much."

"Nonsense. Everything is ready. I can handle an experienced waitstaff. If I need you, I'll find you."

"But dishing up the plates…"

"I brought my most experienced people from the restaurant and hired temps, remember? Things should run like clockwork."

Gratitude flooded through Marlo. "Are you single, Franco? If not, I'd ask you to marry me so you don't get away."

Franco threw back his head and laughed. "I enjoy working

with Dining with Divas. You may have a difficult time getting me to leave."

Marlo was still saying "thank you" as Jake dragged her off to get dressed.

"I'll be seated while you change clothes," he said. To her surprise, he leaned forward and kissed her on the tip of her nose. "The wedding party will be lining up soon."

"How do you know so much about weddings?" Marlo asked.

"Always a groomsman, never a groom," he said, giving her a gentle nudge in the back to get her moving. "Now hurry. I'll see you at the reception."

Lucy was waiting to help her. The dress slipped over Marlo's shoulder and hips in a luxurious cascade of silk. She turned to have her friend zip up the back.

"It's not fair," Lucy pouted. She observed Marlo's lean arms and legs, her golden, sun-kissed skin, garnered from her hours working with My Own Pony, and short-cropped pixielike hair, which enhanced the long, slender curve of her neck. "You look like a model and I look like a…a…a big hunk of black licorice!"

"Hardly. You're darling."

"That's a euphemism for short, isn't it?" Lucy hiked herself onto her tiptoes for another look in the mirror.

Jenny stuck her head through the door. "We're lining up, ladies…Marlo."

Marlo took a deep breath and told herself to smile. This was Angela's day, and she didn't deserve a bridesmaid who looked like a rain cloud. She wouldn't show that she was feeling sorry for herself just because the most unlikely of her single friends was getting married and the only man she cared anything about was off-limits. Straightening her shoulders and forcing a smile, Marlo glided out to join the others.

The other bridesmaids were chattering like magpies until they spied Marlo. Then their words drifted away as they stared at her in silence.

"What? Have I got a strap showing? Why are you all staring at me?"

"Because you are a vision," Tiffany said. "You're stunning, Marlo."

"Don't be silly, everyone is wearing the same dress."

"We're not wearing it like you are," Becky said. "That dress is *you.*"

It did feel good, after all the fashion disasters she'd worn, she had to admit. She glanced to her side and caught a glimpse of herself in the mirror. At least she *thought* it was her. Somewhere between the kitchen and their gathering spot, a transformation had taken place. She didn't recognize the glowing woman in the mirror.

"I'll have to write Angela a thank-you note," she said lightly, hoping her voice was steady. "Now what are we waiting for? There's a groom out there having a nervous breakdown. Let's get this show on the road."

She didn't remember much about the wedding, she realized later. Halfway down the aisle, marching to Handel's "Largo," she caught sight of Jake. More important, Jake caught sight of her. She saw his eyes widen. Once he gained his composure, his gaze continued to lock with hers. It was as if he were the groom waiting by the altar.

If only, Marlo thought.

There were songs, she recalled vaguely, a homily and vows. The flower girl stepped on her toe and Angela, in a case of jitters, nearly dropped her bouquet. Other than those faint recollections, Marlo remembered nothing other than the expression in Jake's eyes.

Chapter Twenty-Three

By the time Marlo and Lucy returned to the kitchen after the ceremony, Franco was looking wild-eyed and barking orders to anyone who would listen. Servers in black trousers and white jackets were milling about like bees near a hive.

"What are you doing out here?" he demanded. "You are part of the wedding party!"

"Until we get the food out, we're Dining with Divas. You didn't think we'd leave you alone with all this, did you?" Marlo grabbed the apron she'd brought—a large one that covered most of her dress and might have been a circus tent in another life.

"Can I help, too?" a familiar voice asked. They all turned to stare at Jake, who stood in the kitchen door, looking more like groom on the top of the cake than a worker bee.

"That's very sweet, but how much experience have you had waiting tables and dishing food?" Lucy demanded.

"More than you think. I paid for two years of college working as a fry cook in a little restaurant just off campus. I thought the experience of being a working college student might serve me someday. And obviously it has. Do you have an apron for me?

This is an Armani suit, and I'd hate to wear it home covered with salad dressing."

"We need all the help we can get. Time to start serving." Franco cut off any protest either Marlo or Lucy might have made. "Let's go."

Jake was as good at serving meals as he was at everything else, Marlo noted. Better yet, no one in Jake's section seemed to mind waiting for food, at least not the women. They were all happy to feast their eyes on Jake.

Meanwhile, in the kitchen, Marlo found herself accidently bumping into him on far too many occasions. She and Jake worked well together. He seemed able to read her mind just before she was about to speak. It was probably that horse-whisperer thing he had. He understood things without words ever being spoken.

"This is quite a workout," Jake commented, even though there was not a hair out of place on his head.

"Fortunately, we don't have to continue." Marlo nudged him toward the door. "Picking up empty dishes is easier than serving hot food. It's time to sit down."

He caught her by the hand. "I haven't had a chance to tell you how lovely you are tonight. You are as elegant and sophisticated as Audrey Hepburn, as glowing and…"

Marlo's insides lurched as she put a silencing finger to her lips. He was Cary Grant and she was Audrey Hepburn. Oh, how she loved those old movies—and their happy endings.

"You're just accustomed to Sabrina. She's always perfect. I'm considerably more ordinary."

"Is that what you think? That you're ordinary?"

"I'm a realist, that's all." She tugged on his hand, which felt warm and right in her own. "Come, the bride and groom will be speaking soon."

After the mention of Sabrina's name, Marlo kept busy at the

reception, managing to be mostly where Jake was not. It was nearly eleven when he finally cornered her.

"If I had self-esteem issues, I'd think you were avoiding me," he said, holding tight to her wrist so she couldn't skitter away again.

"I'm sorry I've been so busy. You can see it's been crazy here."

"But it came off like clockwork. Now we need to talk privately."

It was not a good idea. Jake's nearness messed with her mind. He made her insides go all goopy and her brain into a glob of cottage cheese. "I don't see that there is anything you need to say to me that can't be said in front of a crowd." Marlo wasn't quite sure from where this mulish attitude had come. Maybe she'd caught something from the stubborn little donkey that was new to My Own Pony.

"Well, I do. You're scheduled to volunteer at the stables tomorrow until six. Plan to stay late. We're not putting this off any longer."

She watched him leave, her own mind spinning with confusion. Though it was right for her to keep her distance, she was incredibly curious about this conversation he wanted to have.

Chapter Twenty-Four

He wasn't going to let her get away with anything this time. At six o'clock, Jake made sure he was at the round pen where Marlo was working. They needed to be done with this.

"Thank you for staying. It's important to me that I understand why you are upset with me."

"I'm not upset with you, Jake. I'm upset with *me*."

As he looked at Marlo, he fought the urge to be lost in those wide, blue eyes. She was an amazing-looking woman and she seemed completely unaware of the fact. That only made her even more beautiful. He tipped his head toward one of the Range Rovers. "Get in." When she hesitated, he took her by the elbow and propelled her toward the vehicle.

"I don't have much time," she warned him, as she tried to drag her boots in the dirt. "I have a date tonight."

"No, you don't. You're a lousy liar, Marlo."

"I'm not lying. It's not exactly with a man, but I do have a date with a movie on television that I've wanted to see."

"Rent it. If you like, I'll rent it for you." Jake put the vehicle into gear and they sped off, leaving a cloud of dust and gravel behind them. He drove halfway down the lane without speaking, before turning off onto a small dirt road that led toward a grove of trees at the far end of a pasture.

"Where are we going? I've never been on this road before."

She sounded nervous, Jake noted. Good. She'd certainly made him nervous lately. He wanted this woman in his life like he'd never wanted anyone before, and she seemed unwavering in her determination to keep him at arm's length.

"To a spot I spent a lot of time at as a kid. No one ever knew where I was, so they couldn't bother me there." He seemed to be driving directly toward a thick stand of pine trees, but as he neared, instead of slowing down, he put his foot on the accelerator.

Marlo covered her face with her hands and involuntarily ducked as branches slapped at the windshield. When she looked up, they had entered a meadow that was an almost perfect circle inside the ring of evergreens through which Jake had driven. It was a beautiful little glade, hidden, green and silent.

Jake swung out of the Rover and lifted a few hunks of wood out of the rear end of the vehicle. He walked over to a stone fire ring and tossed the wood next to it. He watched her as she looked around like a timid doe in the forest.

"What is this place?"

"I told you, it was my hideout when I was a kid. I still drive in here every once in a while to make sure the path in isn't overgrown and to see if anyone else has found it yet, but nothing has ever been touched. I suppose people don't realize that inside this tree cluster there is a clearing like this." He looked at her and added softly, "You're the first person I've even brought in here."

"Surely not, there must have been buddies or old girlfriends." She paused and swallowed before continuing. "Or Sabrina."

"No, just you." Without saying more, he picked up kindling— twigs, birch bark and dry pine needles—and he made them into a small pile in the center of the fire ring. Then he took small sticks and built a tepee around the kindling ball. Methodically, he then took medium-size sticks and formed a square just outside the tepee formation. Finally, he added some large chunks of wood and a few more small sticks to the structure.

Being an Eagle Scout had been useful in a lot of ways. He'd never earned a badge for taming a vapor, however, and that was how Marlo seemed to him these days—present but absent, close but distant, and most puzzling, both chilly toward him and warm. She was a long-legged bundle of contradictions and inconsistencies that he wanted to unravel.

There was a lot riding on this, he realized, probably his whole life.

He was so intent on his work that it allowed Marlo time to study him. She could see the muscles of his back moving beneath his shirt and his broad shoulders tensing and relaxing. So focused was he on his project that he barely seemed to notice when dark hair fell into his eyes and he carelessly wiped it away. Then he took a book of matches from his pocket, struck one and held it beneath the tepee of sticks he'd built. It lit immediately.

"Impressive," Marlo murmured from the bench where she'd sat down. "Now, would you like to tell me why you called this meeting?"

He dropped down beside her on a rough-hewn bench.

"Help me understand you. I have to be educated about what's going on between us. Apparently, I've done something very wrong, and I'm not sure what it is. I know you're avoiding me, but I can't figure out why."

She started to stand but he put his hand on her arm and wouldn't let her up.

"What are you running away from?" Frustration etched across his face.

"You! I'm running away from you!" Couldn't he see that this was tearing her apart?

"Why? You treat me like I have leprosy—no touching, no getting nearer to me than is absolutely necessary, no unnecessary interaction. What have I done?"

Seeing his bafflement, Marlo poured out the long, tedious story of her former engagement, ending with Jeremiah and his other woman, the kind of woman she'd vowed she'd never be. "I care about you more than you could ever know, but you are getting married."

"I am?" Jake's frustration turned to puzzlement. "Who says I'm getting married?"

"Sabrina, of course! I've heard your father and Alfred talk about it, as well. What kind of a woman do you think I am?" Tears filled Marlo's eyes. "I was engaged once. I'd planned to marry—and another woman came along and ruined it all. There's no way on earth I'd do that to Sabrina. I've seen the way she looks at you."

"No, I don't know." She was startled by his tone. "Your vision is obviously skewed by your own past experiences, skewed and wrong. I'm not engaged to Sabrina. I never was and I never will be."

"But she said...she *told* me she was going to marry you!"

"Everything you've done is because you thought I was marrying Sabrina? Backing off, discouraging every encounter? Why didn't you just *ask me* if it was true?"

"Because it all seemed so clear," she ventured timidly. "Sabrina should know." Shouldn't she?

Exasperation washed over him like a scalding shower. He liked to think he was always a gentleman and in control of his temper, and he'd been particularly careful to read Marlo's signals and move slowly, but this woman knew how to worm into every weakness he had.

"Why do you back into everything, Marlo? You'd save yourself a lot of time and heartache if you'd go at things head-on."

"But Sabrina said…:"

"That someday she and I would be married, I suppose." *Sabrina strikes again.* It was his own fault for not putting a stop to her flights of the imagination years ago. It had seemed innocuous at the time—and useful. With Sabrina always playing sentry, he was never bothered with women he didn't have time to get to know. While he'd been building the architectural firm, there hadn't been time for dating. And when he added the work at Hammond Stables, there was barely time for sleep, let alone women.

"Marlo, that's her fantasy. Sabrina has been in love with me since she was a child. She started ordering bridal magazines when she was sixteen. I've never paid any attention. I love her, but I'm not *in* love with her."

Marlo thought back to her conversation with Sabrina in the hospital.

"She loves you. She told me so. And I was afraid that, the way you were acting toward me, that you were turning out to be a man like my former fiancé." Tears flooded her eyes. "I couldn't be a party to that."

"It's not the romantic kind of love she's fantasized about," Jake said calmly, as if he'd thought this out long ago. "It's the way Sabrina thinks and talks, but if push came to shove, even she would admit that it's the family kind of love between a brother and sister that she cares about now. When I was seventeen and she was eleven, she called my high-school girlfriend and told her to 'stay away or else.'" He rolled his eyes. "It took me weeks to straighten that one out." He ran his fingers through his hair, obviously annoyed. "It's happened more than once over the years.

"She's had the idea in her head because Alfred and my father always joked that a Hammond/Dorchester dynasty would exist if the two of us married. Somewhere along the line, the three of them began to take it seriously—and the more seriously they took it, the less attention I've paid. That conversation is a broken record that has played in the background of my life ever since Sabrina was born."

"Why didn't you put a stop to it?" Marlo's face was a mask of puzzlement.

Jake had the urge to massage away her frown, but didn't touch her. He was already in hot water and he didn't need to be scalded. "I did, a few times. They'd be quiet for a while but then it would start up again. I just let it go, because the bottom line is that Sabrina and I won't marry and she knows it."

"But she told me…"

"She's jealous and overprotective of what she considers her territory," Jake said wearily. "Me." He'd never felt so caught off-guard or guilty in his life. "I really had no idea that she'd put you on notice, too."

"Why would you let her do this? You know what's best. *Make* her see clearly! It couldn't be that difficult."

He looked at her steadily. "Have there been times in your life when you've seen your sister do or embrace something that you believe to be misguided? Is there anything you wanted to force her to do but couldn't, not without destroying something special in the relationship? Just because Jenny doesn't behave the way you want her to, do you love her any less?" He knew he'd struck a nerve, by the expression on her face.

Brady. "Well, when you put it that way…"

"Sabrina is the closest person I have to a sister. Big brothers tolerate the guff their little sisters give them. My father and Alfred have always encouraged Sabrina. Those two are the ones who really want us to marry. They actually think that it would be 'good' for Sabrina and me." Jake shook his head sadly. "The fact is that it would be good for them, not for Sabrina and me.

"I can handle myself, but their expectations haven't been fair to Sabrina. There is a fellow named Randy Wills who's been in love with Sabrina almost as long as she's been infatuated with me.

"After Cammi's stroke, Sabrina practically lived at the hospital. Her relationship to Cammi is much like mine was to her—protective and tolerant, an adult sibling to a tag-along in the family. Randy was at the hospital with her almost every day. You may even have seen him there." Marlo nodded thoughtfully as he spoke. "I don't think Sabrina thought much about it at first, but she's begun to realize that he is what she needs in a man— not an independent, overworked, platonic friend like me."

"What made things change? Other than Randy's attentiveness, I mean."

He watched the tension in her begin to relax. He looked straight into her eyes as he spoke.

"This week, Sabrina told me that if an eight-year-old child could have her life change in an instant, then there are no guarantees for her either. She's decided to quit playing the game Alfred and my father have encouraged, and live life on her terms." Jake smiled fondly. "She's a great girl, Sabrina. Confused, possessive and easily influenced, but her heart is good. She's funny, clever and a great dinner companion. Randy's going to have a good—if exasperating—life with her."

"So, just like that—" Marlo snapped her fingers "—it's over between you and Sabrina?"

"There was never anything to be 'over' between us. She just

didn't want to let go of the fantasy. It's been a game for her all along. I'm guilty of not putting a stop to it. Frankly, I had no idea how seriously she took her job as gatekeeper for my life. No woman has ever taken Sabrina to heart like that before."

"Maybe that's one of the problems with this world," she murmured under her breath.

"Of course I didn't take care of Sabrina as well as I thought I did, keeping her close to me, humoring her whims." Jake's dark eyes were beseeching. "Can you understand this, Marlo? Is your family so perfect that no one ever does anything wacky or confusing?"

"Are you kidding? How can I criticize anyone else for doing something foolish or extreme? I suppose it shouldn't surprise me or anyone for that matter, that I even backed into love."

"Love?"

She hadn't meant to let that word slip from her lips, but it was out, and there was no retreating now. "I met you, fell in love with you, thought you were engaged and ran away."

"I tried to tell you a dozen times how I felt about you, Marlo. You wouldn't even let me get the words out of my mouth. It was as if you were moving through life with Plexiglas walls around you. I didn't push it because you were so edgy. I've worked with jumpy horses and know better—I didn't want to frighten you away completely."

"I thought I was doing the right thing," she said softly, "by staying away."

"Maybe you were." He picked up a stick and poked at the fire. It flared up and began to burn more brightly. "If you'd been the kind of woman who ran after me, I probably would have high-tailed it in the other direction." A sheepish grin appeared on Jake's features. "I'm still old-fashioned enough to want to be the pursuer, rather than the pursued. Even my father has begun to see that. He's begun to like you a lot, you know. He's even begun to change his mind about 'this Christianity business' because of you."

He shook his head and sighed. "I was actually about to rethink that notion of being the pursuer, the knight in shining armor who'd sweep you off your feet, when I discovered just how hard you were to catch."

Marlo's head reeled with what he was saying, with the possibilities it presented. Still, she didn't move toward him. He didn't like being pursued, but she did. It would make them both happy if he were the seeker and she the treasure.

Jake snapped his fingers and jumped to his feet. "I have some things in the car for you." He went to the Ranger Rover and came back with a box and an envelope.

He put them on the ground in front of her. "Open the letter first. I have no idea what it says."

Marlo didn't recognize the handwriting. The penmanship was feminine. She tore open the envelope. Jake leaned over her shoulder and they read it together.

Marlo—

I'm sorry I gave you such a hard time. I love Jake so much that I've never thought anyone was good enough for him (except me, of course, ha-ha!) But you are first-rate, through and through. I realized that when we visited at the hospital. If I can't have him, then I think you might be the one to whom I'd entrust my sweet "big brother." If he loves you, that is. I want nothing but the best for the man who is my champion, protector and first love. Please accept my apologies for how badly I treated you. You terrified me from the first minute I met you. I suppose I knew you were a woman who could take Jake away from me. Little did I know that you were actually the one woman I could trust not to!

Randy and I are more suited to each other anyway. He's been wonderful throughout Cammi's crisis. I think I'm falling in love with him. Time will tell. Of course, there will never be anyone like Jake ever again. He's definitely worth loving.

Someday I hope we can be friends—
Sabrina

She looked up. "I had no idea."

"I didn't either." A soft smile graced Jake's lips. "Sabrina's always told me everything—until now. But you won her over."

"You are a very tolerant man, Jake Hammond."

"It comes with years of practice. First my father and his idio-syncrasies, then Sabrina and training unbroken horses, and now…" he hesitated "…there's you." He pointed at the box at her feet. "Open it. I've wanted to give this to you for a long time but never thought the time was right. You made it pretty clear that you didn't want me around."

"Shhh. I don't want to talk about that anymore. When I back into things, I can't see where I'm going. Like with you."

She opened the box and her expression grew puzzled. It was a small, black plastic lump that resembled a tiny television with a cord. "What is it?"

"A navigating system for your car so you won't get lost."

She picked it up and a card fell out of the box. She laid the navigator on her lap and opened the card. This one was in Jake's strong hand: "Here's something to make your days a little easier, at least in the car. If you'd let me, I'd like to help you find your way through the rest of your life, as well—Jake."

"It's about time," Marlo said softly, thinking of the List lying on the dresser in her bedroom. "I've been waiting for you forever."

She couldn't—didn't want to—say more. She closed her eyes as Jake's loving kiss touched her lips.

An excellent *kisser. Check.*

Epilogue

M arlo turned slowly in front of the mirror, again checking her sophisticated, white silk dress. Its simplicity heightened the garment's restrained elegance and was likely be the most restrained thing about the next few hours. Jake had insisted on a wedding celebration unlike any other, and with Lucy, Tildy and Franco's help, Marlo thought they just might pull it off.

This wedding was definitely the most untraditional, the members of the Bridesmaid Club agreed, as they primped and preened in the women's restroom facility in Hammond Stables' indoor arena. Each attendant had chosen her own brightly colored garment, and Marlo felt as though she were surrounded by a cluster of beautiful flowers, each more rich and vibrant than the last.

"Ready, ladies?" Tildy poked her head into the room where the group had gathered. "Everybody is waiting."

Obediently, they trooped into line and to the strains of Bach's "Jesu, Joy of Man's Desiring" exited one by one into the wide-open space of the riding arena filled with people seated in white wooden chairs. Marlo, hanging back, peeked through the door at the scene of her wedding. The fence surrounding the riding area was trimmed with sparkling white lights and miles of white netting. Lavish bouquets of flowers flanked both sides of the pastor's podium, and a white carpet was being rolled down the aisle through the sandlike compound on the floor by two architects-turned-ushers from Jake's firm. His friends in the wedding party were wearing tuxedos that were a little dusty at the hems, but no less elegant. Off to the side waited two restless white horses, hitched to a white carriage, waiting for their moment to carry the bride and groom to the reception hall.

She glanced at one section of chairs, those set aside for the families of children who rode in Jake's program, and was gratified to see they were full. Many of the My Own Pony participants were in attendance. They were family to her and Jake now. Jake's relatives, professional associates and friends had also come out in full force, as had almost everyone who had ever bought or sold a horse at Hammond Stables.

In the front row, her mother looked both pleased and confused. The arena was a far cry from where she'd expected her daughter to marry, and she didn't take her eyes off Feather and Lovey, as the two horses meandered free in the arena. Not only beautiful and bomb-proof, the horses were also snoopy, and more than once had to be shooed away as they investigated the flowers and some of the guests. It wouldn't seem right, Jake had said, to marry in the arena without any horses present, and Marlo had agreed. Still, she'd burst out laughing when she and Lucy drove to the ranch to find every horse in sight festooned with a wedding-white bridle with white carnations woven into the buckles.

Sabrina was with Randy, and the glow on the young man's face was as bright as the one Marlo felt growing in her. *A time to love...* Then the only face she could see was Jake's, suffused with happiness and anticipation.

As she stepped out and linked arms with her father to walk

down the aisle, she glanced at her bouquet where she'd placed a folded piece of paper among the roses. The Cinderella List would walk down the aisle with her today, and then be tucked away until she had a daughter of her own. When her daughter had questions about how her mother and father had met, she would bring it out and tell her the story of how she got her prince.

* * * * *

Dear Reader,

I think horses are some of the most beautiful and amazing creatures created by God. Intelligent, graceful and sensitive, it is no wonder they can be used as a means of therapy for the disabled as well as teamwork training, teaching and coaching. The Greek name for *horse* is *hippos* and *hippotherapy* means *treatment or therapy assisted by a horse.* I am trained and certified in equine-assisted psychotherapy and teaching so it was a special delight to create a hero who shares an interest of mine. Jake Hammond is a handsome, successful architect but his real passion is Hammond Stables, his family's business. As a successful horse breeder, Jake wants to see the stable facility used for something more—as a venue for disabled children and therapists to meet and work.

Marlo Mayfield becomes a volunteer at the facility. Since childhood, Marlo and her sister, Jenny, have played a game they refer to as the Cinderella List, which inventories all the desirable qualities of a true Prince Charming. She believes Prince Charming doesn't exist—until she meets Jake Hammond.

I hope you'll enjoy compassionate, easygoing Jake, big-hearted, quirky Marlo and the horses (and food) that bring them together. I'd love to hear from you. Feel free to write to me c/o Steeple Hill, 233 Broadway, Suite 1001, New York, NY 10279.

Warm wishes,

Judy

QUESTIONS FOR DISCUSSION

1. Marlo cheerfully accepts her imperfections, believing that because God made her (and He doesn't make mistakes) that she is perfectly designed for the job God has for her. What is your attitude toward your own imperfections, limitations, foibles and idiosyncrasies?

2. Marlo persists in being pleasant to Sabrina and Randall even though they don't necessarily reciprocate. Are there people in your life like that? How do you handle it? What is your motivation?

3. Consider the main characters. Who was your favorite? Why? Did you relate personally to any of them? Why?

4. After hearing the story of Cinderella as children, Marlo and Jenny play a game listing all the qualities they want in their own Prince Charmings. Have you ever made a mental list of the qualities you'd like in a mate? What are the most important to you?

5. Because of her own life experiences and disappointments, particularly concerning her first fiancé, Marlo made decisions that changed her behavior and ultimately the course of her life. What experiences have you had that have made you a different person?

6. Marlo is a free spirit who likes to have fun. Consider her beach party. Would you have a party similar to that one? Or are you more like Jake, who gives elegant, sophisticated parties? What would a party that expresses your personality be like?

7. Jake's father is a bit of a curmudgeon but Jake is unfailingly polite and courteous to his dad, the epitome of the commandment to honor one's father and mother. Have you spent much time around a parent or grandparent like Jake's? How have you handled the situation? What works for you? What helps?

8. Because of a painful incident in her life, Marlo is very careful not to encourage Jake romantically. She believes he is involved with the beautiful Sabrina. How would you have handled Jake's relationship with Sabrina if you were Marlo?

9. Marlo's friend Angela is planning her upcoming wedding and insists everything has to be perfect, no matter what. Do you know anyone like this? What is the effect it has on people around them? What is there to be learned from this?

10. How does a friend like Lucy differ from a friend like Angela? Which kind of friend are you?

11. If you had seemingly unlimited funds like Jake and could spend it on anything that would help mankind, what would you do? Why would that be your choice?

12. Are you familiar with and comfortable around horses? If not, would you be willing to get on one of Jake's bombproof variety? What must it be like for a child in a wheelchair who is never able to stand tall to get on the back of a horse that is fifteen hands high? What must go through his or her mind?

One step into the living room and she froze again, pan aloft.

A hulking shape stood in shadow just inside the French doors leading out to the garden veranda. This was not Popbottle Jones. This was a big, bulky, dangerous-looking man. She raised the pan higher.

"What do you want?"

"Annie?" He stepped into the light.

All the blood drained from Annie's face. Her mouth went dry as saltines. "Sloan Hawkins?"

The man removed a pair of silver aviator sunglasses and hung them on the neck of his black rock-and-roll T-shirt. He'd rolled the sleeves up, baring muscular biceps. A pair of eyes too blue to define narrowed, looking her over as though he were a wolf and she a bunny rabbit.

Annie suppressed an annoying shiver.

It was Sloan, all right, though older and with more muscle. His nearly black hair was shorter now—no more bad-boy curl over the forehead—but bad boy screamed off him in waves just the same. He was devastatingly handsome, in a tough, rugged, manly kind of way. The years had been kind to Sloan Hawkins.

She really wanted to hate him, but she'd already wasted too much emotion on this outlaw. With God's help she'd learned to forgive. But she wasn't about to forget.

Will Sloan and Annie's faith be strong
enough to see them through
the pain of the past and allow them to open
their hearts to a possible future?
Find out in THE WEDDING GARDEN
by Linda Goodnight,
available May 2010 from Love Inspired.

Former bad boy Sloan Hawkins is back in
Redemption, Oklahoma, to help keep his aunt's
cherished garden thriving and to reconnect with the
girl he left behind, Annie Markham. But when he
discovers his secret child—and that single mother
Annie never stopped loving him—he's determined
that a wedding will take place in the garden
nurtured by faith and love.

REDEMPTION RIVER

Where healing flows...

Look for

The Wedding Garden

by Linda Goodnight

*Available May 2010
wherever you buy books.*

TITLES AVAILABLE NEXT MONTH

Available April 27, 2010

THE WEDDING GARDEN
Redemption River
Linda Goodnight

WIFE WANTED IN DRY CREEK
Janet Tronstad

HOMETOWN PRINCESS
Lenora Worth

A DAUGHTER'S LEGACY
Virginia Smith

THE MARRIAGE MISSION
Pam Andrews

THE ROAD TO FORGIVENESS
Leigh Bale